RAPID FIRE ATTACK

Tactical Police Force gunner Mojo Mugabe caught the Apache's Sidewinder missile launch flare on his sensors. "Bastard's in the air, Wolfman!"

Pilot Rick Wolff hauled back sharply on his cyclic, pulling the nose of his TPF Griffin chopper into a steep climb directly into the sun. Even with his face shield on full antiglare, he still had to squint from the blinding heat of the bright ball in the sky.

"It's still tracking us!" Mojo yelled into his helmet mike.

"Tell me when to evade!"

Mojo watched his radar for a beat. "Now!"

Wolff chopped his throttle and racked the Griffin over in a sideslip. The missile flashed past them, its warhead locked onto the hot sun.

"Where is the Apache?" Wolff shouted, bringing the ship back upright.

"He's right behind us. Coming fast!"

"Hang on and get ready to shoot!"

CHOPPER COPS

RECON STRIKE FORCE

RICK MACKIN

PINNACLE BOOKS
WINDSOR PUBLISHING CORP.

PINNACLE BOOKS

are published by

Windsor Publishing Corp.
475 Park Avenue South
New York, NY 10016

First Printing: February, 1991

Printed in the United States of America

Chapter One

Medicine Bow National Forest, Wyoming; 23 December 1999

A sleek, dark blue helicopter cruised high over the snow-covered Medicine Bow National Forest on the northern Colorado-southern Wyoming border. In the left-hand seat of the speeding machine, Tactical Police Force Flight Officer Jumal Mugabe scanned the readouts from the sensor bank in front of him. A darkening sky threatened snow again, and the black copilot/systems operator wanted to complete his search pattern before the next storm hit.

"Rack this sucker around, Wolfman," he said to the pilot in the right-hand seat, TPF Flight Sergeant Rick Wolff. "A couple more low passes over that valley and we'll be done with it."

" 'Bout time, Mojo," Wolff said as his gloved hands moved swiftly to put the chopper into a hard banking turn high over the mountains. "I've enjoyed about as much of this shit as I can stand. This is boring, man."

"Bitch, bitch, bitch," Mojo smiled. "You should be glad that we're up here enjoying the scenery instead of being back in Denver freezing our asses off on the flight line. We've got the heat turned up and a beautiful view, what more could you ask for?"

"How about a cold brew, a fire in the fireplace, and some sweet thing nibbling on my ear?"

Mugabe shook his head and laughed.

5

As Wolff sent the chopper screaming down over the tops of the trees, the bright yellow letters U.S.T.P.F. painted on her belly identified the machine to anyone below as a Griffin helicopter of the United States Tactical Police Force, the hard-hitting, frontline troops in the war against crime.

By the mid-1990s, it had become all too apparent that America was losing the war against crime. The best efforts of the existing Federal law enforcement organizations were simply not enough to contain the growing crime wave. The primary reason they had failed was that their efforts were all too often scattered and uncoordinated. Also, under the regulations then in force, Federal and state officials were not organized or equipped to deal with criminal gangs that had evolved into small, well-armed private armies.

What was needed to rid the nation of this cancer was one unified, well-equipped Federal police organization that would combine the law enforcement functions of all of the old organizations under one command. But even more important than that, what was needed was an organization that had the mobility and firepower to take on the criminals in face-to-face battles . . . and win.

Initially there had been a great deal of political resistance to the idea of a Federal police force, particularly from the ranks of the liberals and entrenched corrupt public officials. The battle had raged for months in Congress, but the situation had become critical and something had to be done. The old methods were not working. The fabric of national life was in danger of being shredded by the new barbarians—the crime lords and their gangs. The time had come for the citizens to take control of the country again.

One of President Bush's last official acts at the end of his second term in 1996 had been to sign the Federal Tactical Police Force Act, which created the United States Tactical Police Force. Under the provisions of the act, the TPF was given the authority to preserve the peace and uphold the law anywhere in the fifty United States. They were also given the necessary power to do the job.

The mission that Wolff and Mugabe were flying today,

however, wasn't in the name of preserving the peace and up-holding the law. It was a routine reconnaissance mission in support of local law enforcement agencies.

Over the last few months there had been a rash of unexplained downings of aircraft flying over the Medicine Bow National Forest. Both the Federal Aviation Administration and the local authorities in Colorado and Wyoming had been completely baffled when they tried to find an answer for these fatal crashes. When their lengthy investigations had come up empty, they asked for assistance from the Tac Force and their sophisticated Griffin helicopters.

The muscle of the TPF were the Dragon Flights, the highly mobile tactical units based at the three regional Tac Force headquarters in Denver, Philadelphia, and New Orleans. Within hours of a call for help, four Griffin helicopters, a twenty-man Tactical Platoon, and a headquarters staff with their support and maintenance personnel could be on the ground and in the air dealing with any emergency too big for the local authorities to handle.

With their mobility and massive firepower, the Griffin gunships gave the Tac Force its winning edge in the battle against crime. But cops flying helicopters was nothing new in law enforcement. For the last decade police departments all over the country had employed helicopters for a wide variety of tasks. But there were drawbacks to this system. The choppers, originally designed for civilian use, were expensive to operate, and there was limited space in their airframes to accommodate police radios and electronic equipment. In the late 1990s, however, a spectacular new machine had come on the scene, one that met the particular needs of police work, specifically tactical police work.

When the Cold War died in the early nineties, much of the nation's military high technology was turned to police applications. While this infusion of technology gave police units quite a bit of sophisticated new equipment, the best result was the Bell model 506P Griffin, the first helicopter designed from the ground up specifically for police use.

The Griffin was a sleek machine powered by two small

but powerful 750 shaft horsepower General Electric turbines, pod mounted externally on the fuselage, driving a four-bladed rigid rotor with a diameter of only forty feet. Both the main rotor and the shrouded tail rotor had been designed for noise suppression as well as maximum maneuverability. Not only was the Griffin quick and stable, it was quiet.

With a crew of two, a pilot and a copilot/systems operator, the Griffin could carry up to six people or 1,500 pounds of cargo in the rear compartment. Protective measures built into the ships included backup flight controls, self-sealing fuel tanks, armored nacelles for the turbines and transmission, and an armored crew compartment with a bulletproof Lexan canopy and Kevlar seats. Under normal circumstances, the Griffin was immune to ground fire up to and including 7.62mm armor-piercing ammunition.

The heart of these hi-tech choppers, however, lay in their sophisticated sensors and communications systems, which had been borrowed directly from the military. Using either active infrared or light-intensifying systems, the Griffin could see in the dark under almost any conditions. Working in conjunction with a terrain-following navigation and mapping system, the pilot was able to know where he was at all times, day or night. Three types of radar—infrared imaging, all-frequency electromagnetic radiation detectors, and audiovisual taping systems—completed the ship's sensor array.

All of the Griffin's sensors were tied into the aircrew's helmets and instrument panel, and digital readouts and could be seen either on the helmet visor or on a HUD, "heads-up display," in the cockpit. Digital datalink capability allowed both computer and sensor data to be sent between the Griffin and the Dragon Flight ground stations.

Not only were the Dragon Flight Griffins the hottest thing in the battle against crime, the officers who flew the Griffins were a new breed of police officer as well, the elite troops of the elite of Federal law enforcement. With the drastic cutbacks in the American military forces at the end of the Cold War, the men who would have become hot rock fighter jocks in an earlier era were now flying Griffins for the Tactical Police Force.

These were the new "Top Guns" of the late '90s. Young, quick, and fearless, the Griffin air crews saw themselves as the first line of defense against the nation's new enemies, the criminal elements who threatened law and order in the United States. And their confidence was not misplaced. They were hot pilots and they flew the hottest rotary winged flying machines ever designed.

But that was not how Wolff and Mugabe felt today. The job they were doing was less than exciting. They were making a routine sensor search, and the data they were gathering was being sent back to the Western Regional Headquarters of the TPF at Denver to be analyzed later.

Regardless of what Mojo thought about the stunning view of the snow-covered mountains and forests, it was a boring job, and the two flyers would be glad when it was over and they could return to their base in Denver. Christmas was only a few days away, and following that would be the biggest celebration of the millennium, New Year's Day of the year 2000. Both men had hot dates lined up for the history-making party, and they were eager to get started on the preliminary activities.

Even the criminals and drug lords were taking a break for the festivities, and the TPF team was looking forward to a few days of relative peace and quiet. First, however, they had to finish their sensor sweep of the forest and make the long flight back to Denver.

"Did you get your place cleaned up for the party?" Mugabe asked.

Wolff laughed. For him, living in a messy apartment had been developed into a fine art; he actually seemed to go out of his way to trash the place. Mugabe often accused his partner of changing girlfriends every time he needed a new housekeeper. "Dana said that she'd straighten the place up for me."

"Has she rented a dump truck?"

* * *

Six miles from the Griffin, a massive door camouflaged to look like a rock face opened in the side of a mountain at the southern end of the national forest. In the middle of the opening an unusual device appeared. It looked like a large, complex dish antenna mounted on a surplus antiaircraft gun chassis. In reality, it was a directed electromagnetic pulse generator.

The effects of electromagnetic radiation had been discovered during nuclear weapons tests in the late sixties. Remote-controlled aircraft sent in close to gather data about the atomic blasts had suddenly gone out of control and crashed. The wreckage of the drones had been recovered, but all the investigators could discover was that the computerized flight controls had suddenly failed. Closer examination of the aircrafts "black boxes" revealed that something had fried all the transistors in them. Further investigation showed that the "something" was a powerful burst of electromagnetic energy that had been generated at the moment of a nuclear detonation.

This phenomena was quickly named an electromagnetic pulse, or EMP, and frantic efforts were made to examine EMP's effects and to try to find a way to shield modern military equipment from them in case of a nuclear war.

In short, the EMP destroys transistors. Since all modern electronics are transistorized, it can fry anything from a teenager's ghetto blaster to the complex electronics of a combat aircraft. And since everything from radio navigation to fuel management on modern aircraft is controlled by electronic black boxes, EMP can kill an unshielded airplane as effectively as a laser-guided air-to-air missile.

Efforts were also made to try to harness the power of EMP to create a defensive weapon. Creating a low-powered EMP was no problem. But the energy needed to produce the power to make it effective as a weapon required the detonation of a small nuclear device, so the project was dropped. At first, no one thought to try using less power and to focus the lower-powered EMP while boosting it in the way that a laser uses enhanced light beams to burn through steel.

Once that idea was hatched, however, it required only a short engineering exercise to build a directed EMP weapon. That weapon was now aimed at Wolff and Mugabe's Griffin, just as it had been aimed at all the other aircraft that had gone down over the Medicine Bow National Forest over the last several months.

The EMP weapon tracked the distant Griffin for a minute or so, hummed for a few seconds, and was still again.

The massive camouflaged door slid back into place, and once more the mountain looked like a mountain.

Wolff had just completed his last low-level pass and had climbed back up to cruising altitude when Mugabe's radar threat warning indicator sounded, a shrill warbling shriek in his helmet headphones.

"Wolfman," he said with a puzzled voice. "Someone's tracking us on radar."

Wolff snapped his head around. "What?"

"We're being tracked," Mojo repeated, his fingers racing over the sensor controls. "We've got a radar lock-on."

Suddenly the Griffin's sensor screens went dead; the constant throbbing whine of the twin GE T-700 turbines died as well.

"Mojo!" Wolff shouted. "We've lost power!"

With her turbines dead, the Griffin silently plummeted like a stone toward the snow-covered forests below.

"Hang on! We're going down!"

Chapter Two

In the cockpit of the plummeting Griffin, Wolff struggled to regain control of his powerless craft. When the engine cuts out on a fixed-winged aircraft, it does not necessarily mean disaster. Usually the pilot can put the aircraft into a glide and retain some control over his descent. The wings continue to generate lift and can keep the plane in the air for a while. A helicopter, however, has no wings. The aerodynamic lift is generated entirely by the spinning rotor blades, and when the engines die, so does the lift.

A helicopter with her engines dead quickly assumes the glide angle of a falling rock.

Unlike most helicopters, the Griffin had small stub wings on each side of the fuselage, but they were designed only to generate enough lift to overcome the added weight of the weapons pylons the craft carried; they could not help the machine glide when the turbines were dead.

Wolff's only hope was to try to establish autorotation. At best, however, an autorotation was not much more than a semicontrolled crash. There are easier ways to commit suicide than trying to autorotate a helicopter.

But even that slim chance was quickly fading. Being a modern, state-of-the-art aircraft, the Griffin's flight controls were all "fly-by-wire." The input from the pilot's cyclic and collective controls as well as his rudder pedals were translated to electronic impulses and transmitted to the control servos by wires. This allowed greater control and faster flight attitude changes than the old hydraulic control systems, but it also required electronics to operate. When the EMP had blasted the Griffin's electronics, it had also destroyed the fly-by-wire flight controls.

Wolff struggled with the collective for a moment, but it felt like the stick was embedded in concrete. "Mojo, I can't control her!"

"Hit the emergency backup!" the copilot shouted.

Wolff hit the switch activating the backup compressed air hydraulic system and felt the stick pressure ease off. "Got it!" he yelled.

Now to try to autorotate.

With the turbines out, the Griffin's transmission had automatically declutched, allowing the rotor to spin free. This gave him a little lift, but the resistance of the air was slowing the blade's rotation. Wolff carefully eased down on the collective control, flattening the still-spinning rotor blades. This cut the drag on the rotor blades, but it also cut the lift he had been getting from them.

With his eyes fixed on the rotor RPM indicator and the rate of descent meter, Wolff nudged the cyclic stick forward, dropping his ship's nose and increasing her angle of dive. Now that the main rotor wasn't generating lift, the chopper fell faster and sent the air rushing through the blades, spinning them faster and faster.

The loss of power had also cut out the Griffin's multibladed, antitorque tail rotor. But as long as their airspeed stayed above eighty miles an hour, the chopper streamlined itself, and he didn't really need the tail rotor control unless he tried to change direction. If, however, their airspeed fell below eighty miles an hour, the chopper would start spinning like a top from the torque of the main rotor.

As the rotor RPM came back up from the speed of his dive, Wolff started easing up on the collective, turning the leading edge of the rotor blades into the air again to try to establish autorotation.

The veteran pilot didn't need to watch his instruments for this maneuver—he was flying solely by feel. This was where his thousands of hours behind the controls of choppers was going to pay off. If he fed in too much collective, the blades would stall out and stop turning. Too little collective and they would fall much too fast.

As Wolff fought to control their crash, Mojo sat calmly in the left-hand seat of the doomed chopper and watched the ground rushing up at him. If there was anyone in the Tac Force who could keep them from splattering themselves all over the winter landscape below, it was his old buddy the Wolfman. There was nothing he could do to help, so he might as well sit back and wait to see if he was going to die.

The autorotation slowed the Griffin's descent enough that the ground didn't look like it was flying up to meet them. They were still falling, but at a controlled rate. Wolff had time to look up to see if he could find a place to put his ship down safely. However, the snow-covered forest below them didn't offer much in the way of clearings. All he could see in their flight path was an unbroken sea of tall trees.

"We're going into the trees," he shouted.

Mojo tightened his shoulder harness without a word as he watched the forest come closer. No matter how good a pilot Wolff was, putting a chopper into the trees was always bad news. He and Wolff had gone down before, but there was no way that they were going walk away unscathed from this one. This one was going to hurt.

Wolff kept close watch as the tall trees rushed up at them. At the last possible second, he jerked up hard on the collective, pulling full pitch to the rotor blades, and hauled back on the cyclic to pull the nose up sharply. The rotor bit into the cold mountain air, giving him every last possible bit of lift as the Griffin plunged into the forest with her nose held high.

The landing skids caught in the branches first and ripped away from the ship's fuselage. Next, the stub wings sheared off several treetops before they too parted company with the rest of the airframe. Then the tail boom came off with a snap just aft of the rear compartment. Finally, the rotor blades splintered and went flying off in four directions as the cockpit section glanced off a massive tree trunk and rolled down the hillside. It finally stopped, coming to rest on its left side.

When the last chunk of the Griffin hit the ground, there was silence in the forest. The only sound was the rising wind singing through the towering trees and the hooting of a startled owl.

In the Dragon Flight Operations Center in Denver, TPF Sergeant Ruby Jenkins glanced up at her control console and noticed that she was no longer receiving the sensor data input from Wolff's-Griffin. She punched in a code on her keyboard and discovered that the signal had been cut off. She frowned as she checked again on the unlikely chance that she had made a mistake.

Ruby Jenkins was the brains and voice of Dragon Control, the operations center for the Griffins of Dragon Flight. A small, trim woman in her fifties, Jenkins was affectionately known to the men and women of Dragon Flight as Mom, but she was not anyone's idea of a mother. She always had a ready shoulder to cry on, but she also used the vocabulary of a Marine drill instructor and had a quick boot in the ass for anyone who screwed up "her" Tactical Police Force.

Mom ruled her electronic kingdom with an iron hand, but right now her kingdom was not working properly. She was not getting her sensor data from those two aerial cowboys, Mojo and the Wolfman. She clicked in her throat mike for the command radio.

"Dragon One Zero, Dragon One Zero, Dragon Control," she radioed. There was no answer.

"Dragon One Zero, this is Control, come in, please."

Her only answer was a faint hiss of static.

Mom spun around in her chair to face the air control radar operator. "Where the hell have Wolfman and Mojo gone?" she asked.

The radar operator was new to her job and hadn't quite gotten used to Mom's brisk manner yet. "Ah . . . ," she hesitated. "The last time I saw them, they were flying right on the Wyoming border."

Mom frowned. "What do you mean, the last time you saw them? Where the hell are they now?"

The radar operator studied her screen. "Ah . . . They seem to have turned off their transponder."

Mom came out of her chair like a shot. Wolff was an aerial cowboy, but he was also the best damned chopper jock in the entire Tac Force. He would never have turned off his radar transponder on a routine flight. And if he had gone tactical for some reason, he would have reported it.

"Let me see," she shoved her way in front of the radar operator. She scanned the glowing green screen in vain for the blip marked "TPF D-01." "Shit!"

Spinning back around, Mom raced through the operations room for the office of the Dragon Flight commander, TPF Captain J.D. "Buzz" Corcran. The stocky, balding officer was reading through a thick maintenance report when Mom burst into his office. "Wolff and Mugabe are down."

"What!" Buzz jerked his head up. "Where?"

Mom shrugged. "I don't know. They're off the air and we've lost their radar plot."

"Show me."

If there was anything that sent Buzz Corcran into immediate action, it was having one of his ships go down. A chopper pilot himself, he was well aware of the dangers of flying rotary-winged aircraft.

Buzz had first flown helicopters as a young, hot rock, Huey gunship driver with the 1st Air Cav in the Vietnam War. He had picked up his nickname when he had made a high-speed, low-level run over Division headquarters at An Khe after a very successful mission. Unfortunately, he had made his run right over the general's personal latrine, and the general had been on his throne when the rotor blast blew it over. The young Lieutenant Corcran had been lucky

16

that he hadn't spent the rest of his tour picking up North Vietnamese cigarette butts on the Ho Chi Minh trail.

With two tours in the Air Cav and four Purple Hearts under his belt, Buzz had finally decided that he needed a less exciting occupation. He resigned his commission from the army and went into the helicopter maintenance business in Southern California. After a year of that, though, he was bored out of his mind and longed for a little more excitement in his life—specifically, aerial excitement. He answered an advertisement for helicopter pilots for the California State Highway Patrol, but cruising up and down the crowded LA freeways looking for speeders wasn't exciting enough for him either. After a few years, he joined the Federal Drug Enforcement Agency as a pilot.

Flying for the DEA had been much more fun, particularly when President Bush's war on drugs had heated up. He had led the first contingent of DEA gunships into Columbia and Peru to do battle with the cocaine barons and their private armies. Corcran had been in his element there, fighting drug guerrillas in the jungle.

When the Tac Force was formed in 1996, he transferred over from the DEA and had been chosen to command the first Dragon Flight. He enjoyed running his unit, but he resented being deskbound most of the time. He was still a pilot at heart, and each year he somehow managed to wrangle enough hours behind the controls of one of the Griffins to keep his flight status active. The only time that he didn't like running Dragon Flight was when something like this happened.

A quick glance at the air traffic radar screen confirmed Mom's information, and Buzz reached for the radio microphone. "Dragon One Zero, Dragon One Zero, this is Command One, come in, please." A faint hiss sounded over the external speaker and he turned back to Mom.

"Who do we have in the air?" he asked.

"No one," she answered. "Everyone else is down because of the storm warning."

"Who's on ramp alert?"

17

"Gunner and Legs."

"Get them in the air with a paramedic team ASAP."

Mom slid back into her chair, "Yes, sir."

While Mom was contacting the ramp alert chopper, Buzz went back to the radar screen and had the operator play back the last plot for Wolff's Griffin. "They were last seen on the Wyoming border right inside the national park boundary," he told Mom.

"I've got it," she answered curtly.

"What's the flight time to that area?"

"Two and a half hours with the wick turned up all the way," Mom replied.

Buzz frowned. "Try to get someone from the Wyoming and Colorado state police up there right now," he ordered. "It'll take too long for Gunner to get on the scene."

"Right, and I'll alert the nearest hospital."

Buzz turned back to the radar operator. "What's the weather condition up there?"

"The National Weather Service has posted a snowstorm warning for southern Wyoming and northern Colorado," the operator answered.

"Was Wolff informed of this?"

"Yes, sir," she answered. "He said that since they were already there, they might as well finish the job."

"Shit!" Buzz muttered as he slowly shook his head. Wolff was a damned good pilot, but sometimes he let his mouth run away with his ass. This time it looked like he had really stepped in it.

"Keep on it," he growled as he turned back for his office. "And keep me informed."

Chapter Three

A bitter cold rain swept the chopper pad outside the TPF headquarters building in Denver. As soon as night fell the rain would turn into snow. In the right-hand seat of his Griffin, Flight Sergeant Daryl "Gunner" Jennings impatiently watched the chronometer on the instrument panel, his finger curled round the start trigger for the turbines.

In the left-hand seat, his copilot/systems operator, Flight Officer Sandra "Legs" Revell, stared out through the rain-spotted canopy in front of her. Some of the rain drops were now falling as sleet. They had no business trying to fly in weather like this, but Rick and Mojo were down somewhere. And if they were down, there was nothing that the crews of Dragon Flight wouldn't attempt to get them back.

Gunner finally triggered the switch to his throat mike. "Dragon Control," he radioed. "This is One Four, what's the holdup? Let's get this show on the road."

"This is Control," came Mom's raspy voice over his helmet earphones. "Keep it in your pants, One Four. I'm clearing your flight now. You're go."

" 'Bout time," Sandra muttered as she started through the turbine startup checklist. As Gunner's gloved fingers flew over the Griffin's switches and controls, he called out

19

each item to his copilot.

"Internal power, on. Inverter switch, off. RPM warning light, on. Fuel, both main and start, on. RPM governor, decrease. Portside starter, engaged."

Legs looked over her shoulder to check both sides of the ship. "Rotor's clear. Crank it!"

Reaching down with his right hand, Gunner twisted the throttle open to "flight idle" and pulled the starting trigger on the collective control stick.

In the rear of the bird, the portside GE T-700 turbine burst into life with a screeching whine and the smell of burned kerosene. Over their heads, the forty-foot main rotor slowly began to turn, moving faster and faster. As soon as the portside turbine was running at forty percent RPM, he switched over and fired up the other one.

As the turbine RPMs built up and the rotor blades came up to speed, the pilot held the throttle at flight idle and watched the exhaust gas temperature and RPM gauges. Everything was in the green.

He twisted the throttle all the way up against the stop. The whine built to a bone-shaking scream as the turbines ran up all the way to 6,000 RPMs. Everything was still hanging in the green zone.

He flipped the RPM governor switch to "increase," and the turbines screamed even higher at 6,700 RPMs. Everything was still green.

Gunner backed off on the throttle and clicked in his throat mike. "Control, One Four, taking off now."

"Control, copy. Good luck."

Cracking the throttle open again, Gunner gently hauled up on the collective, lifting the Griffin off the helipad in a low ground effect hover. He nudged down on the rudder pedal, swinging her tail around to line up with the runway. Twisting the throttle all the way up against the stop, he pushed forward on the cyclic control. The chopper's tail rose and she started down the runway in a classic, nose-low, gunship takeoff.

As soon as his airspeed came up, Gunner hauled up on the collective, pulling pitch on the rotor blades. Her turbines screaming at maximum revs, the sleek, dark blue machine leaped up into the dark winter sky, her rotor blades clawing the cold moist air. As soon as Gunner cleared the Tac Force airfield, he banked away to the north and climbed for cruising altitude.

As the paramedic team in the back settled down for the long flight, Gunner peered through the canopy at the low-hanging clouds. It looked like it was going to be IFR, instrument flying, all the way.

Daryl "Gunner" Jennings was the son of a Vietnam gunship pilot who had died late in the war. He had still been an infant when his father was killed in action. A few years later, his mother married an ex-gunship pilot turned cop. As a boy, he had been raised on old chopper gunship war stories and grew up watching video copies of the classic Vietnam war movies. His favorite was *Apocalypse Now*, with it's stunning vision of a blazing "airmobile" helicopter assault. He had watched that scene so often that he was on his second laser disk copy of the old film.

A minor heart murmur had kept him out of military service, but it had not been bad enough to keep him from joining the TPF and graduating from the Griffin flight school. The Tac Force wasn't the military, but so far duty with Dragon Flight had given him several opportunities to fire his chopper's guns in anger, and he was always eager to open up on the bad guys every chance he had—hence his nickname.

He wasn't planning to get into a shootout today, but considering the weather, this flight would be dangerous enough without it.

Sandra sat quietly behind her sensor and weapon controls, her eyes flicking from one readout to the next. Her face was composed but her mind was racing, and it was difficult for her to concentrate on navigating for her pilot. Rick Wolff was down somewhere in the wilderness, and she and the Wolfman went a long way back.

The first day that Sandra had shown up for duty at Dragon Flight, a smiling Rick Wolff had sauntered up to her and asked her for a date. Trying to make a good first impression, she had patiently explained that she didn't date the men she worked with.

"Great," he had laughed. "Since you're not flying with me, we can have dinner tonight."

She had been sorely tempted by Wolff's boyish good looks, his deep green eyes, and his easy smile, but she had gone on to explain to him that she was serious about not dating anyone in the force. He had just smiled, slowly running his green eyes up and down her frame.

"Okay, Legs," he had said. "I'll catch you later on the flight line."

The nickname had stuck and so had her determination not to go out with him. It had soon become a ritual with them. Every couple of weeks he would ask her for a date, and every time she would turn him down. Sandra's rigid rule about not dating the men she worked with was her insurance that she wouldn't be taken for just another thrill-seeking bimbo playing games in a man's job. And even though under other circumstances she probably would have fallen for the dashing pilot's line, she made no exceptions to her rule, not even for the Wolfman.

Sandra Revell had worked hard to get where she was, and she wasn't about to take any shit from anyone, on or off the force, about being a woman cop. She had never turned down an assignment, no matter how tough, and she had never complained when the men tried to make her lose her temper or quit. Whenever she got any shit from one of the men, she just waited patiently until the next hand-to-hand class and then proceeded to kick his ass up between his ears.

As a result, Sandra Revell was well respected around Dragon Flight, and most of the men she worked with seemed to have forgotten that she was a woman. A few of them, however, stung by her refusal to play along with their macho games, had started a rumor that she was a lesbian. She really didn't care what they thought, but she had to admit that her love life had suffered since she had joined the Tac Force. Too many of the men she dated had figured her for an easy screw just because she was a woman cop.

Even her most recent relationship, a short affair with a Mexican police pilot on their last mission on the Gulf Coast, had not turned out well. She thought she had finally met someone who took her seriously, but he had turned out to be working for the enemy, and she had been forced to kill him in an aerial shootout.

When she had gone into a brief tailspin over that one, it had been the Wolfman who had talked her down from it. Even though she had always kept Rick at arm's length, time and again he had been the one friend she could always count on in a crisis, any crisis.

On top of that, Sandra remembered all the things she had learned about flying from Wolff. Like the time that he had flown off her wing over the Pacific, guiding her back to land after her pilot had been killed. They had been intercepting a shipload of drugs, but the ship had been armed with heavy antiaircraft machine guns. The same burst of fire that had killed the pilot had also knocked out most of the flight controls, making it almost impossible for her to keep the Griffin in the air.

But Wolff had flown alongside her ship all the way back to land, talking her through it, coaching her in all the tricks he had learned from his countless hours behind the controls of a chopper. He had told her little things about flying that had never been printed in any flight manual, things that had kept her from crashing into the ocean. She certainly owed him for that incident, and several more as well.

* * *

In the snowbound forest, the figures in the shattered wreckage of the Griffin stirred. "You okay?" Wolff asked, turning to his gunner as he shrugged out of his shoulder harness.

"I think so," Mugabe answered slowly.

"Where the hell are we?"

"I don't know," Mojo said, wincing as he leaned forward to scan his readouts. "All the screens are dead and the backup power is out."

Even with the ship's main power off, the standby batteries should have cut in to maintain enough power to run the screen readouts, the radio, and the navigational maps for several hours. Whatever had gone wrong with their Griffin seemed to have fried all of their electronic gear.

"Try the radio."

"I did," Mojo shook his head. "It's dead too."

"Fuck!"

"I think the location beacon is out too," Mojo added.

"For Christ's sake, what happened?"

Mojo shook his head again. "I don't know, man. It's like lightning hit us or something. I can't get anything to work."

Wolff stared out of the split canopy for a moment, trying to figure out how he and Mojo were going to get out of this one.

Rick Wolff and Jumal Mugabe went back all the way to the inception of the Tac Force Dragon Flight. They had both been in the first Griffin helicopter conversion class and had been assigned to fly together at the start of the weapons training phase. At first, Wolff hadn't known what to make of the muscular black with the gold earring, bushy mustache, shaved head, and jive-ass attitude. But after the first day on the gunnery range he knew that he was working with a master of aerial gunnery, a real left-hand-seat ace.

"Where'd you learn to shoot like that?" he had asked him when they got back to the chopper pad at the end of that first day of training.

Mugabe rocked back on his heels and grinned. "Oh, here and there," he had answered cryptically.

"Here and there where?"

Mojo had flashed a big smile. "Nicaragua, Columbia, Iran, South Africa, places like that."

"Who'd you fly for?"

"U.S. Mail."

"Okay, okay," Wolff laughed. "Why don't I buy you a beer and you can tell me about it."

That night the two men discovered that they had a lot in common besides their love of flying choppers. Wolff had not been able to fly in any of the recent wars, so he was enthralled by Mugabe's combat stories. The burly black gunner had flown for several of the government's secret armies as well as for the CIA and DEA. He had finally gotten that out of his system when he had stopped a bullet in the jungle. After that, he tried civilian life for awhile. Finding that boring, he signed up for the Tac Police as soon as they had started recruiting.

Mojo was interested to learn that Wolff was a hot rock air show and racing pilot who had a restored a World War II vintage F4U-5 Corsair fighter to play with. He immediately volunteered his services if Wolff needed mechanic work done. Among his many talents, Mugabe was also an ace aircraft mechanic, and he loved to work on old warbirds.

When the Griffin school ended, Wolff was the top pilot, and he requested that Mugabe be assigned as the gunner on his chopper. Since then, the two men had worked together and played together both on and off duty. They had been in some pretty hairy situations before, but nothing like this.

* * *

"What do we do now?" Mojo asked.

Wolff looked around the cockpit. Both doors had been sprung open in the crash and the rear compartment had been torn open as well when the tail boom snapped off. A harsh, biting wind howled through the openings. "We've got to get out of here," he said, "and find us a shelter."

"Didn't they always tell us to stay with the crash so they can find us?"

"That's what the book says," Wolff agreed. "But they didn't tell us how we're supposed to keep from freezing to death while we wait. Let's get the survival gear and get the hell outta here while we can still move."

"That may be a bit of a problem," Mojo said slowly. "I think my arm's broken."

Chapter Four

Wolff quickly unbuckled his shoulder harness and leaned over to help Mugabe out of his. "Let's take a look at that arm."

"I don't think there's anything to see," Mojo said between clenched teeth. "I just can't move it."

"Can you get back to the rear compartment?"

"Yeah."

Painfully struggling to get past the two front seats, the gunner managed to reach the troop seats in the rear. "Oh, Jesus," he said softly as he flopped down into the first seat he came to.

Wolff grabbed the ship's first aid kit and kneeled beside him. "Unzip your flight suit."

Mojo opened his flight suit and pulled it down over his left shoulder. As he had said, there wasn't much to see, just a swelling at the shoulder end of his collarbone. He reached up to examine it, but touching it sent waves of pain shooting through his arm.

"I think it's the collarbone," he said between clenched teeth. "I slammed my shoulder against the seat when we crashed."

"I think there's a sling in here somewhere," Wolff said, digging through the first aid kit. "Yeah, here it is."

After checking the rest of Mojo's arm for other injuries,

27

Wolff gently pulled the flight suit back up over his shoulder and zipped it up again. Taking the sling, he braced Mojo's left arm tightly against his side and bound it securely in place.

"That feels a little better," Mojo said. "That should do until we get picked up."

"Speaking of getting picked up," Wolff involuntarily shivered as he tied off the sling, "we can't stay here. We've got to find someplace where we can get out of the wind and build a fire."

A gust of wind blew snow into the rear compartment and Mojo also shivered. "Yeah, let's do it."

Wolff helped his partner into one of the two padded nylon flight jackets they had worn before their takeoff in Denver several hours earlier. They weren't the fur-collar variety flight jacket, but they were better than nothing.

Grabbing the survival kit and the first aid bag, Wolff stepped out of the shattered Griffin into the deep, drifted snow. He turned around and carefully helped Mojo step down. The sudden shock of the cold surrounding the gunners legs made him gasp. "Jesus!" he said through gritted teeth.

Wolff pushed through the snow leading the way down the hill. The chopper had crashed on the side of a gently sloping hill, and in survival school, they had been instructed to always walk downhill. Even with the chill of the wind and the deep snow cutting through him, the exercise started to make him feel warmer. "How you doing?" he asked.

Mojo panted with the exertion and the pain. "You'd better find us a place to camp real soon. I think I'm going into shock."

Wolff looked around them. There was a small gully at the bottom of the hill and a tree who's branches grew close to the ground. It wasn't much, but Wolff thought that he could build a snow shelter using the low-hanging

28

branches for a roof. "Not too much farther," he said. "I think I've found us a place to stay."

Wolff helped Mojo sit down with his back against the tree trunk and quickly got to work packing snow into a wall around them. The thin leather flight gloves he wore offered little protection against the numbing cold, and he soon lost all sensation in his hands, but still he continued working. If Mojo was going to last through the night, he had to build him a shelter from the wind.

In a little over half an hour, Wolff had completed the wall of packed snow on the windward side of the shelter and started sealing off the other two sides. The snow-laden branches overhead made a good roof, and in another half hour the small shelter blocked out the wind altogether. As Wolff had worked, the wind had risen and snow had started falling again. The storm they had seen coming had arrived, but they could survive it now.

"Okay," Wolff said, patting his hands together trying to restore enough feeling so he could open the survival kit from the chopper. "Now let's see about setting up house-keeping here."

When Mojo didn't answer Wolff stripped off one of his gloves and laid the back of his hand against his partner's forehead. Even though his hand was half frozen, he knew that Mojo's temperature was high—too high. His dark skin was unusually pale and there was a thin sheen of sweat on his shaved head.

Wolff slipped his wet glove back on and rummaged through the survival kit for a space blanket, the tough Mylar plastic sheet coated with a shiny heat-reflecting surface on one side and a dull black, heat-absorbing coating on the other. Opening the small packet, he pulled out the thin sheet and wrapped it around his partner with the shiny side facing toward him. It would reflect his body heat and cut his heat loss.

Next he took out one of the small cans with a candle

inside and, placing it next to Mojo, lighted the wick. Survival candles were small, but they would burn for almost six hours, and the specially formulated wax gave off a great deal of heat. Once the small candle was burning, it became almost warm in the shelter. Like the space blanket, the packed snow reflected the available heat.

The next thing on the agenda was dinner. Neither one of them had had anything to eat since breakfast, and the cold was rapidly sucking the energy out of them. Wolff went through the survival kit, brought out one of the survival meal bars, and opened the foil package.

"Here you go," he said, shaking Mojo awake and handing him half of the survival bar. "Dinner."

"I'm not hungry," Mojo mumbled.

"Come on, man," Wolff urged. "You've got to eat. You need the calories to keep warm in this cold."

Mojo took the bar and munched on the dry, tasteless, high-calory mixture. "This tastes like dog shit."

"Freeze-dried dog shit."

Mugabe finished his dinner and snuggled back down into the hollow in the snow he was lying in. He was asleep in seconds. Wolff reached over and laid his hand on his gunner's forehead again. It was burning hot now. Shit! Shock and fever both.

The wind howled outside the makeshift shelter as Wolff wrapped the space blanket tighter around Mugabe. If someone didn't show up soon and get them out of this mess, they were going to be in a world of hurt.

Bad news travels at the speed of light in a police unit, and Dragon Flight was no exception. No sooner had Gunner and Legs lifted off than the unit's off-duty personnel started filtering into Dragon Flight's unofficial rumor-control headquarters, the maintenance officer's cubbyhole office in the front of the maintenance hanger.

Eric "Red" Larsen, Dragon Flight's maintenance officer, was a big, burly, soft-spoken man who looked every one of his fifty-odd years. It was easy to mistake him for a teddy bear kind of guy, but the greying remnants of his once flaming red hair served as a warning of his fiery temper.

Red's love affair with helicopters had begun back when he had been a young chopper mechanic in Vietnam. When he got out of the army, he started working on police choppers, and now, almost thirty years later, he was still in love with rotary-winged flying machines.

When the Griffin was still on the drawing boards, Red had been brought in as a consultant to explain to the Bell design team what a real police helicopter ought to be, as only a man of his years of experience would know. Since his input had been incorporated into the final design, Red considered the Griffins to be his children, and woe be unto any young hotshot pilot who abused one of his birds. In addition to his job as the flight's maintenance officer, he was also the crew chief for Wolff's Dragon One Zero, just so he could keep his hand in the actual work on the ships.

Since it was his personal Griffin that was down somewhere in the woods, Red Larsen was not at all happy. He was chomping the end of his dead cigar furiously as the men and women of Dragon Flight started filtering into his office to get filled in on the latest rumors.

Red's crowded office was in its usual state—complete chaos. Grease-smudged work orders and maintenance updates littered his desk. Cigar butts overflowed from two ashtrays, one on each side of the desk. For a man who was so meticulous about his work, he lived like an animal, and a sloppy animal at that.

Everyone who came in walked directly over to the huge army surplus coffee maker sitting on top of a rickety old filing cabinet and helped themselves to a cup before finding a place to stand around Red's desk. If the Environmental Protection Agency ever raided Red's office, his brew would be condemned as a Class One hazardous chemical. But it was hot, and drinking a cup of it was a requirement for joining the crowd. Anyone seen not drinking Red's coffee would be unceremoniously thrown back out into the rain.

The maintenance chief had a speaker on the wall that was surreptitiously hooked into Mom's commo network. Everything that went out over the command radio was piped into his office so he could keep track of what was going on. It was, of course, a serious violation of communications security, but no one had the balls to tell him to take it down. Red was going to keep informed no matter what, and to hell with asinine security regulations.

One of the first officers to stop by Red's office was TPF Lieutenant Jack "Zoomie" Zumwald, the Tactical Platoon leader. The Tac Platoon was Dragon Flight's ground combat unit, a platoon-sized SWAT team, the other half of the hard-hitting chopper cops force. Although he was basically a ground cop, Zoomie had many good friends among the Dragon Flight pilots and crew. In a business like theirs, there was no place for the ground forces-air forces rivalry of traditional military units. When any one of the chopper cops was in a bind, it was the same as if it was one of his own men.

"What's the word?" he asked Red as he sorted through the collection of dirty cups around the coffee pot, looking for one that was even halfway clean. The one he finally picked was stained a deep muddy brown from caffeine, but it least it didn't look like a rat had shit in it. He filled the cup only half way. He knew the rule about the coffee, but he didn't want to kill himself today.

Red shifted the dead cigar butt to the other side of his mouth before answering. "SOS, same old shit. Mom's still trying to get the Sky Spy surveillance satellites on line to look for them, but the weather's blocking their view of the ground and they can't see shit."

"How long till Gunner gets up there?"

Red glanced up at the clock on the wall. "Another forty-fifty minutes."

"Jesus."

Zoomie took a tentative sip of the hot coffee and almost spit it out. "Christ, Red! Don't you ever clean that fucking pot?"

"Why should I?"

"This shit tastes like battery acid, that's why." Zoomie grimaced.

"I thought you Tac Platoon people were real men," Red sneered. "Not a bunch of pussies."

Zumwald shut up and' drank his coffee. When Red was worried about one of his birds, he could get real testy, and Zoomie didn't want to find his young ass thrown out on the wet tarmac.

"This is really great stuff, Red," Zumwald grinned broadly. "You should try burning it in the turbines when we run out of JP-4."

"Smart ass."

"Captain," Mom's voice sounded tight over the intercom. "Can you come in here? We've got a problem with One Four."

"Be right out."

Buzz dropped the report he had been reading and raced for the operations room. Mom was at her commo console and she turned at Buzz's approach.

"Gunner and Legs just called in," she said. "They ran into a blizzard and had to put down in a small town in Colorado to wait till it blows over."

"Shit! Where are they?"

"Grimsley," Mom pointed to a dot on the map just to

33

the south of the Wyoming border.

"Also," she continued. "The Wyoming and Colorado state police units have not been able to get into the area either. The storm's got everything nailed down to the ground."

Buzz frowned. "What do the weather people say about the storm?"

"They're expecting it to blow through by mid-morning tomorrow."

Buzz silently tapped his fingers on the desk for a moment. By that time, Wolff and Mugabe would have been on the ground for well over twenty-four hours. A man could freeze solid in less time than that. "Is there any kind of airstrip in that forest?"

Mom called up the map on her computer screen. "It looks like there's a Forest Service water bomber strip here," she pointed.

Buzz studied the map for a moment. "Alert the flight," he ordered. "I want all three birds, a jump CP, full support facilities, and the Tac Platoon up there the moment the weather clears. Notify Washington that I'll be leading the flight up there myself."

Mom hesitated for a moment. "It's Christmas Eve tomorrow, Buzz," she said.

"I know. Ask for volunteers from the bachelors if you have to, but I want to get someone up there ASAP. If those guys are still alive, we've got to get them out of there before they freeze to death."

"We'll get them back, Captain."

"We'd fucking better," Buzz growled. "I've got a lot of time invested trying to make real cops out of those two hot dogs."

Chapter Five

Las Vegas, Nevada; 23 December

A good-natured crowd of several hundred people had gathered in the plaza in front of Caesar's Palace in Las Vegas. Even this late in the year, it was a balmy seventy degrees in the desert resort town, and the people were dressed as if they were attending a spring festival. It was a young crowd, most of them were in their twenties and thirties, but several were well on their way to senior citizen status. The only thing they had in common was that everyone wore a deep green armband on their right sleeves.

An elevated speaker's platform had been erected by the main entrance to the famous gambling casino, and the crowd was cheering the man standing behind the microphone and the bulletproof Lexan security panels. Flanking him on each side of the platform were larger-than-life posters of the man's smiling face. Bold green lettering at the top and bottom of the posters proudly proclaimed, "Clean Earth Party — Buck Sloan in 2000."

Behind the crowd, network television vans focused their cameras on the speaker — financial genius, inventor, and Las Vegas businessman Benton "Buck" Sloan — as he wrapped up his speech announcing his candidacy for the office of president of the United States. Unlike the traditional candidate's speech that seemed to go on forever without saying anything, Sloan's words had been short and to the point. Not once had he slipped into the professional politician's grab bag of hackneyed phrases and buzzwords. He had spoken like a rational man, and that was what the crowd had gathered to hear.

When the last echoes of his amplified voice faded, the crowd roared their approval and surged forward chanting "Buck! Buck! Buck!"

Buck Sloan stood with his arms raised over his head for several minutes, letting the noise and adulation wash over him, an open smile plastered on his face. Finally he lowered his arms and stepped off the rear of the platform. Secret Service agents quickly surrounded him as he stepped back through the front door of the casino and quickly walked across the lobby to the elevator.

Sloan didn't relax until the massive doors to his penthouse office on the top floor of the building slid shut behind him. "Christ!" he muttered softly, shaking his head. "What a mob." He walked over to a plush sofa and sank into the cushions.

"You're the one who wanted to go into politics, Benton," Jordan Mattiese, his campaign adviser, reminded him, carefully keeping his voice neutral.

"I didn't know that I'd have to wear this damn flak vest," he said, shrugging out of his bright green sports coat with the Kevlar bulletproof lining.

"The Secret Service people insisted on it," Mattiese said. "Like it or not, now that you've thrown your hat in the presidential ring, they're calling the shots on your personal security."

Sloan shook his head wearily. "Who the hell'd want to shoot me?"

Mattiese smiled grimly. "Oh . . . I can think of a dozen or so guys who'd love to see you dead and buried, Benton. And that doesn't include the media freaks who just want to get their names in the news."

Sloan turned to his manager. "Jordan," he said. "I told you to call me Buck, even when we're alone. It's part of the image."

"Sure, Buck."

Jordan Mattiese had been part of the East Coast Democratic party political establishment before he took over Sloan's campaign, and he was still not used to the practiced informality of Sun Belt politics.

Sloan would rather have had a campaign manager from California, but his backers had insisted that he use Mattiese and had gone to great expense to buy the experienced political manager away from his old party loyalties. Mattiese was good at what he did, and even if he was still learning to conduct a campaign Western style, Sloan was making steady headway in the polls. If it continued that way until November, he'd be the next president.

Sloan hadn't formed the Clean Earth party, but then Hitler hadn't started the Nazi party either, and both men had quickly risen to the top of their adopted organizations. Sloan wasn't the explosive leader that Hitler had been, but his wealth had given him instant access to the party, particularly since much of his money came from his work on solar energy power sources.

Buck Sloan was the archetypical Sun Belt success story of the late nineties. With the disintegration of American society in the northeastern states over the last decade, the center of American business and industry had moved to the southern and western states. The exodus away from the Northeast had been led by the new hi-tech industries seeking room to grow in a social environment free of chronic crime, urban collapse, and endless labor union violence.

As the year 2000 approached, the Sun Belt stretched from Georgia to the Pacific, except, of course, for Los

Angles and the Southern California area, which had been completely abandoned by industry in the late nineties.

Sloan was a big part of America's shift in economic base. Riding the crest of the wave, he had turned an electrical engineering degree from Cal Tech into a multimillion-dollar financial empire known as SOLCO. As the name implied, SOLCO was based in large part on Sloan's pioneering of solar energy sources.

Another great part of his wealth, however, came from shrewd manipulation of the stock market. Sloan had the reputation of being almost clairvoyant when it came to the market. His trading was so accurate that the Securities Exchange Commission had investigated him for insider trading fraud, but he had been declared clean. He hadn't really been clean, but his trading information came from a source that could never be traced. A source that the SEC would never even have thought of.

While working on a way to improve his own worldwide communications systems, Sloan had discovered a way to tap into the satellite network that serviced the world's business affairs. All companies use encrypting devices to scramble their communications, but Buck had developed ways to decode them. His brilliant moves in the stock market were based on the information he gathered from these clandestine communication interceptions.

Mattiese was completely unaware of this other side of Sloan's life, he only knew his boss as a slightly eccentric millionaire who had attracted the attention of certain East Coast moneyed families. He didn't quite understand why they had chosen Sloan to be the next president, but they had and they were willing to make Mattiese a millionaire to see that it happened. For that reason alone the campaign manager was willing to do anything it took to put Buck Sloan in the White House. If he had to, he was even willing to call him Buck.

38

"Your next performance," Mattiese said, consulting his pocket computer notes; "is scheduled for tonight at the annual meeting of the American Association of Administrative Scientists."

Sloan leaned back and put his hands behind his head. "What the hell do they want to hear?"

"The usual," Mattiese answered. "But for those people, you need to stress jobs and management in the emerging alternate energy business."

"Draft it up and I'll go over it later."

"I'll get right on it," Mattiese said, standing up and turning to go.

Buck stood up and walked over to the window to look down at the crowd still clustered in front of the casino. Las Vegas cops in full riot gear were hovering around the fringes of the group waiting for even the slightest excuse to move on the crowd. Sloan was a native son, but that did not mean that the established political structure in Nevada welcomed him with open arms. In fact, the two major parties had put their traditional differences aside so they could join forces against what they saw as a serious threat to their continued political existence. But so far, it didn't seem to be working.

The Clean Earth party was quickly gaining strength, not only among the oat bran and wood stove set, but also among middle-of-the-road Americans who were truly concerned about the environment. Unlike the earlier radical environmental groups like Earth First! and the Euro Greens, the Clean Earth party had a workable, common-sense platform. There was none of the technology-hating Luddite hysteria and return-to-the-Stone-Age thinking that had characterized earlier attempts to put environmental concerns into a political platform. These people had a program that sounded rational.

In fact, the most radical stand of the Clean Earthers

was that they wanted to see an immediate end to the use of nuclear power plants and a rapid phaseout of oil- and coal-fired plants as well. With the massive Gulf Coast oil spill back in October, people had become alarmed and the party's strength had tripled almost overnight. That strength was still growing by leaps and bounds, and it was going to put Buck Sloan in the White House.

Most of this strength was in the Sun Belt, but since the congressional and electoral college redistribution after the 1990 census, the South and the West finally had enough political clout to take control of American politics. If the major parties did not band together to stop Sloan, it would be the biggest disaster in American political history.

The Republicans were concerned because they were the dominant party and wanted no opposition. The Democrats were in a state of panic because they saw the new party as cutting deeply into their already steadily vanishing ranks. If the Clean Earth party won the next election, the Democratic party would cease to exist except as a footnote to American political history.

Both major parties were doing their best, but their problem was that Buck Sloan was the most perfect candidate for president the country had seen since Teddy Roosevelt. He was a self-made millionaire and had apparently made his money cleanly. There was a little rumbling about his part ownership in a gambling casino, but that didn't cause concern in the Sun Belt. Not when the front-running Democratic presidential candidate had publicly confessed to anti-Vietnam War rioting and dope smoking, was supported by suspicious Latin American interests, and was on his fourth blonde bimbo starlet wife. The Republican candidate was a little more acceptable, but he was colorless and considered not too bright. If the man had to ask his bitch goddess wife which tie to wear, how could he possibly run the country?

Compared to traditional American politicians, Sloan was a breath of fresh air. He was open and plain speaking, a man of the people. He had been married, but was now a widower, and he did not chase women. He dressed Western casual in cowboy boots, sport coats, and Western hats, and did not behave as if he were above the common people he was asking to vote for him. He always appeared poised when he was on camera and he always seemed to speak from the heart.

Old women loved Buck Sloan, and the young saw him as a bright sword raised against an establishment that was corrupt beyond redemption. If things kept going the way the polls pointed now, he was a shoe-in for the White House.

Which was, of course, exactly what his political backers wanted. Sloan was rich, but he was not rich enough to cover the expenses of a presidential election out of his own pocket. Certain East Coast interests who wanted to move their enterprises from the urban decay of the Northeast were backing Sloan's play. If he won, they expected that certain executive decrees would be made that would grease the skids for them so they could make their move. Considering the vast amounts of money they were pumping into Sloan's campaign and the Clean Earth party, there was no way that he could refuse to return the favor once he was in office.

Sloan was a man of the people, but he was not naive. He knew that his real backers were old-time mob families turned respectable who wanted to make a new start in the West. He knew and he didn't mind at all, because their plans fit right in with his. He knew that when he hit the White House he would be on the road to amassing riches beyond his wildest dreams.

And if he knew how to do anything, Buck Sloan knew how to dream big.

41

He turned away from the window, sat behind his polished oak desk, and activated the computer monitor. Before Mattiese came back with the bullshit he was to deliver to the Administrative Scientists tonight, whoever they were, he wanted to check in with his clandestine satellite communications interception facility hidden in the mountains of southern Wyoming.

Sloan's Project New Dawn was scheduled to kick off on New Year's Day, less than a week away now. He knew that everything was on track, but he wanted to check in just to make sure. He had not gotten where he was by not checking all of the details. Particularly when it came to something as big as this.

Sloan smiled tightly. If the politicians thought they were having trouble with the Clean Earth party now, just let them wait till New Year's Day of the year 2000. When Project New Dawn went down, the whole country was going to belong to the Clean Earth party.

The screen came alive and Sloan entered his identification code word.

Chapter Six

Staying at the Bed-A-Bye Inn in Grimsley, Colorado was like stepping into the Twilight Zone for a quick trip back to the late '60s. Gunner and Legs would have preferred to stay a little closer to their chopper and its radios, but accommodations in Grimsley were few and far between. So, they and the paramedics had left the Griffin parked at the small airstrip outside of town and had taken rooms in the rundown motel, the town's only pretention to tourist accommodations.

The phones in the rooms went through a manned switchboard in the front office, and Gunner had been burning up the lines back to the TPF headquarters in Denver. He knew that the drunken old biddy who ran the place was listening in on his conversation to Mom and Buzz, but they weren't discussing sensitive information, so it really didn't matter. It was hard to get your jollies in a place like Grimsley, so Gunner was willing to give the old gal a thrill.

Placing the black phone receiver back on its cradle, Gunner stared for a moment at the print of an obscure impressionistic painting of Venice hanging crookedly on the stained wallpaper over the lumpy bed. It buggered the mind to think that somewhere in the United States people actually made a living reproducing bad prints of mediocre

43

paintings, mounted them in cracked, fake wood plastic frames, and then sold them to motels throughout the nation. It was his experience, however, that a motel had to be at least twenty years old—and sleazy—to be allowed to purchase such a rare print to adorn its rooms.

He repressed a momentary urge to run out, knock on doors, and inspect all the other rooms in the motel to see what great works of art adorned their walls. Actually, it would make a great article for the *New Yorker* magazine, "Motel Art of Middle America."

Not that Gunner actually read the *New Yorker*. His reading tastes ran more to *Police Firepower* and *Hustler*. But he felt that someday he should at least look through one copy of the *New Yorker*. After all, the late-night movies he watched on Turner Network all carried the *New Yorker*'s advertisements. "The best magazine in America," they called it. "Maybe the best magazine there ever was." That might be true, but Gunner didn't think so. He didn't like the artsy-fartsy covers, and the ads he had seen never indicated that the magazine carried any articles on police work or firearms, so he had not bothered with it. Maybe when he retired from the force he would read a copy just to say that he had done it, but right now he had far more important things to do.

He had to go talk to Legs and see about getting something to eat. He was starving.

Sandra Revell toweled her long blonde hair dry. The next time she went out on an emergency mission she would have to remember to pack her hair dryer in her flight bag, she thought with amusement. Now she knew why so many women had cut their hair short in the days before the invention of hair dryers. She shook her long mane out behind her to let it finish drying in the air.

She was just stepping back into her flight suit when she heard a knock on the door. "Just a second," she called out,

44

pulling the front zipper up. "Come on in."

Gunner opened the door just in time to catch a flash of a bulging black lace bra as it disappeared behind the harsh police blue of the flight suit. That uniform sure as hell looked better on her than it did on anyone else he had ever seen wearing it. He stopped short. "Sandra?"

"Yes?"

"Ah . . . Both of the paramedics have crashed for the night. You want to grab something to eat?"

She tossed her head, swinging the half-dry mane of thick blonde hair to one side. "Sure," she smiled. "I'm hungry enough to eat the asshole out of a skunk."

Gunner laughed. Sometimes he thought his copilot spent a little too much time hanging around with the boys. "I don't know if I'm quite that hungry yet," he said, "but the manager said that we could get something to eat across the street at a place called the Dead Owl Bar and Grill."

"Is that some kind of loggers hangout?" she asked.

Gunner shrugged. "Damned if I know," he answered. "But she said that it's the only place in town that's likely to be open this late."

"The Dead Owl it is then," she replied, pulling on her flight jacket. "How cold is it out there?"

"It's cold enough to freeze the proverbial brass nuts off a steel bridge," he answered.

Sandra checked the clip in her .32 caliber Beretta semiautomatic pistol and reholstered the weapon on the back of her belt. As far as real stopping power went, the Beretta was of little use unless the small rounds hit exactly where they were aimed. But Sandra didn't mind; she was a dead shot, which made the Beretta perfect for a backup piece. Plus, it was a comfort to feel the cold hard steel nestled against the smooth curve of her hip.

"Let's go."

It was a short walk across the windswept street to the Dead Owl Bar and Grill, but the driving snow made it seem more like an Arctic expedition. Even with the streetlamps, it was difficult to see more than a few feet in front of them. They navigated across the street by watching the blinking red Coors beer sign in the window.

Opening the door of the Dead Owl brought a blast of warm air loaded with the rich aromas of yesterday's chili, wet socks, and stale beer. It was a familiar smell and Gunner felt right at home. Legs took a deep breath and followed the pilot into the bar anyway.

Gunner went right up to the bartender. "The manager of the motel across the street said that we could get something to eat here," he said.

The bartender was a heavyset man with a wild shock of hair and a full beard and was wearing a plaid wool shirt, a typical native mountain man. He gave Sandra the eye and focused on the Dragon Flight patch on the left breast of her flight jacket. "You two cops or something?"

"Federal Tac Force out of Denver," Sandra answered. The tone of her voice made it clear to him that she wasn't going to book any shit from this guy about it either.

"Sure," he said, smiling thinly. "We've got burgers and fries and chili and fries."

Gunner ordered a bowl of chili and Sandra had a cheeseburger. Both ordered a glass of Coors draft and took the beer to one of the tables to wait for their food. As they sipped their beer, Gunner looked around the dimly lighted room. Surprisingly, there wasn't a skier or snow bird in the crowd. All of the customers had that hard, weatherbeaten look of Rocky Mountain natives.

"Nice place," Sandra said, looking over the top of her glass as she took a sip of her beer. "Friendly people, great atmosphere. It goes well with the motel and the rest of this dump."

46

"It ain't beautiful downtown Denver, that's for damned sure."

Gunner was used to being the center of attention every time he went out in public in his Dragon Flight gear, but this was not the usual curiosity. Most of the people in the bar looked overtly hostile, as if they were hiding something. He tried to tell himself that it was his imagination, but his cop's instinct for trouble was on full alert.

Sandra felt the same way. There was something about the way the men were looking at her that made her want to reach for her pistol. Particularly those four guys at the table closest to the back door. One of them was staring daggers at her and Gunner, but she shrugged it off. Maybe the guy had done time or something and had a hard-on at cops. As far as she was concerned, that was just tough shit. She was hungry and didn't care what his problem was.

The food came quickly and they both dove into it. Sandra was halfway through her meal when the man at the back table stood up and walked over to the jukebox. He dialed up a country and western song, something slow with a guy singing mournfully about his long-lost divorced wife. The man then crossed over to their table and walked up to Sandra. "You wanna dance?" he asked.

Sandra put her burger down and looked up at him, but before she could speak, Gunner cut in. "No, she doesn't."

The man looked over at Gunner. "I wasn't talkin' to you, cop," he slurred. "I asked the lady cop."

"No, thank you," Sandra replied. "I don't dance."

The man smiled. "I'll show ya how," he said, reaching for her arm.

Sandra twisted away from his grasp and was on her feet in a flash, her arms at her side in a fighter's stance. "Move on," she said.

Gunner struggled to push his chair back, but the man

47

clamped his hand down on the back of Gunner's neck and slammed his face into the table.

Sandra exploded into action. Her right leg snapped up, her boot catching the man on the inside of his left knee. The snap of the joint sounded clearly over the music right before he screamed and went down.

With a final kick to the man's kidneys, she stepped back and snatched the Beretta from the holster on her belt. Taking a two-handed stance, she covered the other three men from the back table.

"Call the sheriff," she snapped at the bartender.

From the corner of her eye, she caught a glimpse of the big man coming up from behind the counter with a sawed-off shotgun. Pivoting to the right, she aimed the small pistol directly at his left eye. "Drop it!"

The shotgun fell to the floor.

"Call the sheriff! Now!"

Being careful to keep his hands above the counter, the bartender reached for the phone and Sandra moved back to cover both him and the other men. One of the three had ducked out the back door, but the other two were standing stock still. They were still standing motionless when the sheriff came through the door a moment later. By this time, Gunner had gotten to his feet and was standing beside his partner, blood running down his face.

"What's the problem here?" the sheriff asked, his eyes taking in the scene.

"I want these people booked," Sandra said.

"Now wait a minute, Officer, we can . . ." the sheriff started to say.

"I hope that I don't have any trouble about this, Sheriff," Sandra said, her voice as cold as the wind outside. "The maggot on the floor is looking at two counts of assaulting a Federal officer, and I don't want to have to write you up too for obstructing justice."

The sheriff swallowed. "No ma'am, I'll book 'em."

"Book him and print him," she said. "I'll have a Federal marshal up here tomorrow, and I want to see if there's any outstanding wants and warrants on this asshole."

"You can turn those other two clowns loose," she pointed to the two remaining men from the back table. "And," she continued, pointing to the bartender. "As for this asshole pulling a sawed-off shotgun on me, I want him booked, printed, and held for a little chat about Federal weapons violations."

The sheriff looked very grim now. The bartender was one of his old poker buddies and he had talked to him about that damned gun several times.

"Any questions?" Sandra snapped.

"No ma'am."

Gunner leaned closer to the sheriff. "In case you folks don't get the newspapers up here," he said, pressing his handkerchief against a cut on his cheekbone. "I'd like to inform you that fucking around with the Tac Force is a quick way to find your ass in deep shit. You got that?"

The sheriff nodded.

After finishing his half of the rations, Wolff wrapped the other space blanket around himself, leaned back against the tree, and tried to get comfortable. He knew that he should rest to conserve energy, but he was too wired to sleep, and every time the unconscious Mojo moaned he reached out for him, even though there was nothing more he could do.

For the first time in his life, Wolff didn't have a handle on the situation. He had been in tough spots before, but there had always been something he could do to fight his way out. This time, all he could do was to sit and wait until someone found them.

Since he couldn't sleep, he decided that he should try to do something to better their chances of survival. He really wished that he had paid more attention to the cold-weather survival classes, but during his training he had slept through most of the classes that had not been on the subject of flying.

Shit, he had been training to be a pilot, not some damned skier or mountain climber.

The one thing he did remember from the survival classes the TPF pilots had attended, however, was the need for water, even when it was freezing outside. Dehydration was a serious problem in winter survival conditions. He scooped snow into one of the plastic bags from the first aid kit and, unzipping his flight suit, put the bag next to his skin to thaw the snow. The shock of the cold snow sent shivers through him, but he knew they would have to have the water.

Wrapping the space blanket tightly around himself, he huddled next to Mojo and tried hard not to think of the fur-lined, air force flight line jacket that Red always wore. Wolff had teased the maintenance chief about it, but right now he would have killed for a pair of the coats and the Mickey Mouse arctic boots that went with them. He couldn't remember when he had last been able to feel his toes. Or his fingers either, for that matter.

He rolled back his sleeve and glanced at his watch. It was slightly past six, but the sky was as dark as if the sun had already gone down.

If they weren't found by the next morning, they would have to get going again. The problem was that he had absolutely no idea where they were; the map had been useless to him once they left the downed chopper. The snow flurries had totally obscured the terrain, and there had been no way for him to navigate. The small compass in the survival kit was one of those new electronic types, and it had been fried along with all of the rest of their electronic equipment. For all he knew, they could have been on the back side of the moon.

He checked Mojo again and looked out at the expanse of whiteness surrounding them. The snow was falling heavily now, and not even the tops of the trees could be seen. It was going to be even tougher plowing their way through the new snow in the morning.

Chapter Seven

The disappearance of the downed Tac Force chopper made the morning headlines even in Las Vegas. With Christmas right around the corner, the media tied it into the rest of the holiday season human interest stories. All the Las Vegas channels carried the story on the morning news about the two brave chopper cops lost in the woods. They also reported that Buzz would be moving Dragon Flight's jump CP into the national forest today to look for his missing men. A side comment briefly mentioned that a group of environmentalists planned to protest the TPF operations.

"Damn!" Buck Sloan muttered when he heard the stories on the news. When he had been notified about the downing of the Griffin he had thought that the episode was closed. Just another of the unexplained aircraft disappearances in the area. He never thought that the Tac Force would go to these lengths to get their two men back. He really didn't mind seeing the TPF waste their time running around in the mountains. But with that many people poking around on the ground, there was too great a chance that someone would stumble onto his hidden installation.

And that was the one thing he could not allow to happen under any circumstances. Certainly not at this point

52

in the game, not when New Dawn was just a few days off.

He hit the intercom buzzer on his desk and Mattiese answered instantly. "Did you catch that story about the Tac Force moving into the national forest today to look for one of their choppers?" he asked.

"Sure did, Buck." Mattiese answered. One of the first things he did every morning was to skim through the paper and cruise the news channels for anything that might affect his candidate. In this business, you had to stay informed.

"Good. I want you to get out a press release," Sloan told his manager. "I want it to express the party's support for those people who are going up to protest the TPF base in the national forest."

"Are you sure that you want to do that, Buck?" Mattiese cautioned. "There's a lot of public sentiment for those missing cops."

"I know that," he said. "But the Clean Earth party can't simply stand by while the forest is polluted by snowmobiles and helicopters. There's a lot more at stake here than the lives of those two men. Of course, I want you to put in something about our concern for their lives, but hit heavily on the possibility of major ecological damage from the search teams."

"Yes, sir," Mattiese answered.

"Also, I want you to contact the party office and arrange for some volunteers to be flown up there this morning. I want us to be well represented on this thing."

"Yes, sir," Mattiese said as he released the intercom button.

The campaign manager paused for a moment, his fingers on the keyboard of the computer in front of him. Not for the first time, he wondered why in the hell he had left Democratic party politics to work for this guy. The money had had something to do with it, of course. It had been hard to turn down a flat fee of a million dollars, win or loose. But he was beginning to think that he had made a serious career mistake. Going head-to-head with the Tac Force over something as silly as a few exhaust fumes in the woods didn't make good political sense to him. He didn't mind protecting the wilderness, but this was ridiculous. And there were two men's lives at stake this time.

He sighed and reached for the phone. He didn't like it, but the first axiom in this business was that right or wrong, the candidate was always right.

Gunner and Legs were up at first light to meet Grimsley's sheriff when he came to pick them up at the motel for the short ride back to the airstrip. Gunner had already been on the phone back to Denver and knew that Buzz was sending a task force up to help them look for Wolff and Mugabe. Now Buzz wanted him to fly to the Forest Service airstrip in the national forest and make sure that it was ready to receive them.

On the ride, the sheriff didn't have much to say to the two cops except that he was real sorry about the ruckus, as he called it, in the bar last night.

Gunner, his face bruised from the pounding he had taken against the table, smiled thinly. "No sweat," he said. "The Federal marshal's on his way now to take those two assholes into custody."

"That other guy," the sheriff said. "The one that slammed your head into the table. Well, he ain't really from around here. He lives up in the mountains and just comes to town every couple of weeks to get drunk."

"He won't be getting drunk for a couple of years," Sandra smiled. "And that bartender will be lucky if he doesn't find himself in a cell right next to him. Sawed-off shot guns are a big no-no where I come from."

"I just wanted to let you know that the townspeople

here are real sorry about what happened, that's all."

"It does seem to be a friendlier place this morning," Sandra replied as the car turned into the snow-covered airstrip. "Thanks for the ride."

Stepping out of the sheriff's car, Gunner saw the son of the man who ran the small airfield service standing next to their Griffin, stamping his feet in the cold.

"I topped off your tanks with JP-4," the gum-chewing kid said, holding out a clipboard. "You want to sign for the fuel?"

Gunner scrawled his name and badge number on the fuel receipt. Digging into his wallet, he pulled out a card. "Send that receipt to this address," he told the kid. "And you'll get paid."

"No sweat, mister," the kid said, taking the card. "We do this all the time for the Forest Service."

After a quick walk-around inspection of their ship, Gunner and Legs strapped themselves in the Griffin and fired up the turbines. As soon as the power came up, Gunner keyed his throat mike.

"Dragon Control, Dragon Control," he radioed. "This is Dragon One Four."

"One Four, this is Control Airborne," came Mom's voice from the C-9 high in the sky on her way to the search area. "Go ahead."

"This is One Four, we are getting airborne now. ETA to the airstrip, thirty-four minutes."

"Control, copy. We'll meet you there."

"Okay," Gunner said to Legs as he twisted the throttle open and pulled up on the collective. "Let's get our asses in gear."

With a flash of her rotors, the Griffin lifted off. Circling the small airfield, the chopper climbed up into the bright blue sky and banked away to the north. Buzz and the rest of Dragon Flight were less than an hour behind them.

* * *

The storm slowly passed over the forest during the night, and at dawn Wolff woke up stiff from a night on his frozen bed. He went outside the shelter to take a leak, work the kinks out of his legs, and to check their surroundings. The bright sun revealed an unending expanse of white, broken only by a few trees sticking up through the snow. The sky was clear, but it looked like there were more clouds building up to the west. If they were going to continue on their way, he knew that they had better get started before the next storm hit.

Ducking back into the shelter, he shook Mugabe awake. "Hey! Mojo!" he said urgently. "Reveille! Wake up!"

Mojo's eyelids slowly fluttered open, and Wolff could see the pain in his eyes. "How do you feel?"

The gunner licked his dry lips in answer.

"Want a drink?" Wolff asked.

When Mugabe nodded, Wolff helped him sit up and handed him the plastic bag of the water he had thawed from the snow.

"Thanks," Mojo said after drinking deeply of the flat-tasting water.

Digging into the aid bag, Wolff gave him two aspirin tablets, which he downed with more water. Breaking open a survival ration, he handed Mojo one of the concentrated food bars. "I'm not hungry," the gunner mumbled.

"Eat it, god damn it," Wolff growled. "You need the energy."

Mojo was too exhausted to argue. He chewed listlessly on the tasteless bar, washing it down with more water. "Now what?" he asked. "We going to stay here?"

Wolff shook his head. "I think we'd better get moving again. We'll freeze if we stay here. Do you think you can walk?"

Mojo nodded slightly. "Yeah."

Wolff quickly packed up their survival gear, scooped more snow into the bag to thaw, and helped Mojo get to his feet. Putting his arm around his partner's shoulders, Wolff led him through the thigh-deep snow. If they just kept on heading downhill, sooner or later they were bound to run into something or someone who could help them. He also knew that if they didn't find help they would probably freeze to death sooner or later. But if they stayed in the shelter, they were sure to freeze to death that much quicker.

They had been on the move for a little less than an hour and Mugabe was fading fast. Wolff was holding him up as they plowed through the snow, and the additional effort was rapidly taking its toll on him, too. Maybe he had been wrong, maybe they should have stayed at the shelter.

Through a break in the trees, Wolff suddenly spotted the regular shape of man-made construction a few hundred meters ahead. Squinting against the almost overpowering whiteness around him, he saw what looked to be a small cabin built against the hillside. The roof was covered in several feet of snow, and no smoke rose from the small chimney, so it was obviously abandoned. But it was a shelter and would let them get in out of the cold.

Since there was a chimney, there had to be some kind of a stove or fireplace inside as well.

"Hey," he said. "I think I've found someplace we can stay."

Mojo muttered an inarticulate response. Holding onto his partner, Wolff stumbled on through the snow.

There was no lock on the cabin door, and when Wolff pushed it open he saw that the shack was in fact deserted. It looked like no one had stayed in it for a very long time. It was as cold inside as it was outside, but at least

57

they were out of the wind. There was a bed frame and a rusty potbellied stove in the middle of the single room. It sure as hell wasn't the Hilton, but the two men were in no situation to be choosy.

Dragging Mojo inside, Wolff laid him on the bed. The exhausted gunner fell asleep instantly. Wolff tucked the space blanket around him and took stock of their surroundings. The first thing was to see about building a fire.

There was a small pile of mildewed hunting magazines by the back of the stove, and Wolff immediately started crumpling the pages as he looked around to see if there was any firewood. There was none, but there *was* a solid wood table on the other side of the room and two wooden chairs around it. He wasn't planning on having too many sit-down meals there, so they would do nicely.

After placing a large pile of crumpled paper on the dead ashes inside the stove, he grabbed one of the chairs and started snapping the legs off. The wood was bone dry and he knew that if he could get the paper to burn, the wood would go in a flash too.

Wolff carefully placed the pieces of the broken chair on top of the paper and dug into the survival kit for the waterproof matches. The paper caught on the first match and the flame quickly spread. "Come *on*," Wolff muttered as the small flames licked the wood. "Light."

As soon as the chair caught fire, the flames spread rapidly, and before long there was a blazing fire in the stove and he could feel the air grow warmer. Wolff pulled the bed frame closer to the stove and pulled the space blanket away from the side of his unconscious partner to let him soak up the radiant heat.

Wolff then pulled off his wet gloves and carefully dried them by holding them in front of the flames on a piece of the chair back. The fire burned so well that it was soon warm enough for him to take off his flight jacket. But see

58

ing how fast the dry chair burned, Wolff knew that he was going to have to find more fuel. Tipping the sturdy table over, he kicked one of the massive legs loose and fed it to the flames. It caught immediately and was soon burning as fast as 'the chair.

Coming from an urban background, the pilot didn't know enough about wood stoves to realize that if he closed the door and shut down the damper on the flue he could slow the burning and make the dry wood last longer. All he knew was that the crackling fire felt good and that watching the flames made him feel warmer than the actual temperature in the room.

As soon as the first table leg was more than half gone, he broke another one off and added it to the roaring flames. He spotted a rusty cast iron teapot and took it outside to fill with snow. There were bouillon concentrate tablets in the survival pack, and when Mojo awoke, Wolff could make a hot chicken soup from them.

As he placed the pot close to the stove to melt the snow, he spotted a small hatchet on the floor by the makeshift shelves nailed on the back wall. In minutes, the shelving had been reduced to firewood as well.

Stacking the wood close to the stove, Wolff thought that if he sat and carefully fed the wood into the fire one piece at a time, he might be able to make it last for maybe two hours. But that was not going to keep them alive very long. As soon as the wood was gone, the temperature would fall quickly.

Wolff looked around the small cabin for anything else that might burn. But except for the rest of the table, all that was left were the walls and the floor, and he couldn't start taking the flooring up, that would only let more cold air in. The only thing to do was to take the hatchet outside and see what he could find for firewood in the forest.

Mojo was still sleeping, so he stuffed another piece of wood on the fire before putting his flight jacket back on.

59

He also took the Glock pistol from his holster and stuck it in his side pocket just in case he saw something to shoot for dinner. The survival concentrates would give them energy, and while they were good as hors d'oeuvres, a roasted rabbit would make a real satisfying entree.

Chapter Eight

Medicine Bow National Forest; 24 December

Wolff pulled on his dry gloves, zipped up his flight jacket, grabbed the hatchet, and stepped out into the cold air. After spending over an hour in the warm cabin, the cold hit him like a hammer. He turned up the thin collar of the flight jacket and tried not to think of fur-lined parkas with hoods as he sank up to his knees into the powdery snow.

The woods were only fifty meters away and he vaguely remembered seeing a downed tree on his way down to the cabin. It would be a hell of a lot easier to chop a piece off of a dead tree than to try to chop down a live one. He was supposed to be a chopper pilot, not some kind of god-damned logger.

He felt his feet start to go numb again as he pushed his way through the drifted snow. Chopping wood should warm him up a little, at least until he could get back to the potbellied stove.

A faint sound reached his ears. He stopped dead and listened, but heard nothing more. It had almost sounded like an engine. He scanned the skies looking for moving black specks that would be aircraft searching for them, but the sky was clear. He shrugged his shoulders and started walking toward the trees again. It must have been something in the woods; maybe the wind was rubbing two branches together. The snow muffled sound anyway.

There was a small dead tree at the edge of the woodline, just as he had remembered from their trip to the cabin. He pulled it out of the snow and tried to drag it away, but it was too heavy. He stopped tugging when he realized that he would have to cut it into at least two pieces before he could move it. Then he could drag it back to the cabin and chop it up into smaller pieces where it was warm.

Pushing the trunk back down, he hefted the hatchet and, picking a spot several feet down from the top, started chopping away at the trunk. Wolff chopped furiously, but it seemed like the small hatchet had last been sharpened sometime during the Vietnam War. It took several whacks to cut even a small chip of wood off. At this rate, it was going to take an hour to cut through it.

They only good thing about it was that the exertion made Wolff feel warmer than he had felt outside for the last two days. He even felt himself break out in a light sweat. He paused for a moment and looked at the rather small pile of wood chips at his feet. Now he knew why he had become a pilot instead of a lumberjack. This was hard work. He raised the hatchet again for another whack.

"Put the ax down! Now!" a man's voice rang out from behind him.

Wolff spun around, the small hatchet still in his hand, as a figure on snowshoes wearing a hooded white snow camouflage suit stepped out from behind a tree. The man was cradling an assault rifle in his arms with the muzzle pointed straight at him.

"I said drop it!"

Wolff dropped the hatchet and raised his hands. "Take it easy," he said, his mind racing.

"What are you doing here?" the man snapped.

"We crashed our chopper," Wolff replied, trying to sound calm. "And we've been in the woods for two days. My partner and I . . ."

At the mention of Mojo, another man stepped out into the open from behind the tree. He too wore snowshoes and

62

a snow camouflage suit, but he carried a holstered pistol on his waist. "Check out that shack," he ordered as he drew his pistol and aimed it at Wolff.

"Hey! Wait a minute!" Wolff said as his hand went for the Tactical Police Force ID badge in his breast pocket. "We're cops."

"Freeze!" the man with the pistol snapped.

The muzzle of the gun lined up with the center of Wolff's chest didn't waver, and the pilot decided not to press his luck. He halted and put his hands back up in the air.

What in the hell had they run into?

"Stand facing that tree," the man ordered, pointing the pistol behind Wolff. "Put your hands on it as high up as you can reach and spread your legs."

Wolff had no choice but to assume the position. Keeping the muzzle of the pistol trained on him, the man quickly patted him down. First he took the Glock from the pilot's side pocket and put it in his own belt. Then, finding the TPF ID badge in his breast pocket, the man glanced at it and put it away in his pocket.

"Okay," the man said as he backed off, keeping his distance from Wolff. "You can turn around now, but keep your hands up over your head."

"I told you we were cops," Wolff said. "We need your help."

The man looked at him for a long time, the expression on his face unreadable. "Let's go down to the shack," he said finally, motioning with the pistol.

Wolff led the way back down the hillside to the cabin. The door was open, and when they entered, Wolff saw that the man with the rifle was standing over Mojo. The gunner was still unconscious. He moaned softly when the space blanket was pulled away from him.

"This one's in bad shape," the man with Mojo said after he had patted him down. "He's running a pretty good fever and he's shivering."

"What's wrong with him?" the man who appeared to be

the leader asked Wolff.

"He broke his arm in the crash," the pilot replied. "He needs to see a doctor."

"What were you two doing up here, anyway?" the leader asked. "According to your ID, you're from Denver."

"We're from Denver all right, Western Regional Tactical Police Force Headquarters," Wolff said, thinking fast. "We were on a winter flight qualification mission up to Cheyenne."

The man frowned and Wolff wondered if his lie was going to be believed. Instinctively, he knew better than to tell this guy the real reason they had been flying over the forest. He didn't know if there was a connection between these guys and the downed aircraft, but he was willing to bet the farm that there was some kind of connection here.

The man with the pistol took a small radio from his belt and spoke softly into it. When he got a muffled answer, he clipped the radio back onto his belt.

Three more men in snowsuits soon appeared at the door of the cabin. Two of them carried a litter on a sled and the third had an extra pair of snowshoes and a heavy parka cradled in his arms. "Put these on," the man said curtly, handing them to the pilot.

"Where are we going?"

"You'll find out when you get there, asshole," the man with the pistol said. "Until then, keep your fucking mouth shut."

While Wolff quickly slipped into the welcome parka, the leader turned to one of his other men. "Sanitize this place before we leave," he said.

"Right."

Wolff's heart sank when he heard the order. Sanitizing the cabin meant removing all signs that they had ever been there. What in the fuck was going on here?

The two men with the litter lifted Mojo onto it. They wrapped blankets around him before strapping him down securely and taking him outside to the sled.

"Okay, let's get going," the man with the pistol ordered Wolff.

"Where are you taking us?" Wolff tried again.

"Like I said," the man snapped, "you'll find out when you get there. Move it!"

Wolff walked out and was immediately surrounded by guards as the small party headed directly for the woods. Once they were well under the cover of the trees, they started moving uphill. A quarter of a mile further on, Wolff saw several snowmobiles parked under the trees. That was what he had heard earlier.

Obviously, his captors had parked the machines there so they could approach him silently. This situation was getting weirder by the minute. Who *were* these guys? Whoever was in charge of this operation was running it like a first-class military exercise.

The men quickly transferred Mojo's litter to one of the machines and tied Wolff's hands behind his back before sitting him in the passenger seat of another. When they fired up the engines, Wolff was surprised to find that they were well muffled and made little more than a hum as they headed east, keeping well out of sight under the trees.

When the snowmobiles broke out of the woods half an hour later, Wolff saw that the man on the lead machine was headed straight toward a dark spot on the side of a snow-covered mountain. As he got closer to it, he saw that it was some kind of an opening in the side of the mountain, maybe an old mine shaft.

The snowmobiles were quickly driven into the mine shaft, and by the light of their headlights, Wolff saw a parking bay with fuel stores in a side chamber around the first bend of the tunnel. Without a word, the men parked the machines and dismounted. The leader of the group then led his captives farther back into the tunnel, lighting his way with a powerful lantern. They continued for a hundred meters or so before the man stopped. Wolff heard a whining noise, and a door opened from what looked like a side tunnel revealing an elevator.

Entering the elevator car, Wolff noticed that there were no controls, only a keyed slot. The leader slipped a key into the slot and the door slid shut as the car moved backward as if on rails. A few seconds later it came to a sudden stop and then started rising slowly. Wolff counted the seconds, but since he had no idea how fast they were moving, it didn't mean anything.

The car stopped and the door slid open onto a brightly lighted hallway. Two men dressed in dark blue coveralls and holding submachine guns at the ready stepped away from the wall and covered the elevator as Wolff stepped out. The men carrying the litter started off down the hall, and Wolff followed them without being told.

A few meters on, the man with the pistol swung open a metal door and pointed to the room inside. "In there," he ordered.

The narrow room looked like an unused storage area — bare concrete walls and floor, a single light bulb in a fixture high on the ceiling, and a steel door with a padlock on the outside. It was small and bare, but it was more than adequate for a holding cell.

The men placed the litter on the floor and backed out. As the door closed behind them, Wolff heard the sound of a padlock being snapped through the hasp.

While Gunner and Legs circled their Griffin over the Forest Service airstrip high in the mountains, the first of the Tac Force's dark blue C-9 cargo planes touched down on the snow-covered landing strip. The instant that her wheels were in contact with the ground, the rear ramp door started opening. By the time the C-9 hit the end of the strip and turned around, the ramp was all the way down and men scrambled out.

Red Larson was the first one out the door, pausing only long enough to light the stub end of a well-chewed cigar clamped between his teeth. "Assholes and elbows!" he yelled to the other men, some of whom had stopped to look around at the frozen winter paradise. "All I want to see is assholes and elbows! Get that pallet outta there! Now!"

The men stopped their gawking and got to work offloading the plane and stacking the boxes and cartons in the snow. Several men carried a folded Army GP Large tent and started setting it up right alongside the snow-covered runway.

As soon as the first plane was unloaded, a second C-9 landed and disgorged her cargo as well. In the hold of the second plane were a dozen dark blue snowmobiles bearing the yellow markings of the Tac Force. They were fired up and driven off to the side of the airstrip to wait for Zoomie's men, who were now circling overhead in the third C-9, waiting for the runway to clear.

The last C-9 touched down, and it too was offloaded in minutes. In slightly over half an hour, Dragon Flight was on the ground and going into operation even as the third C-9 took off for the flight back to Denver. The C-9 was no sooner out of sight before the rest of Dragon Flight's Griffins appeared over the strip.

Now that Dragon Flight was all here, Gunner and Legs brought Dragon One Four in and settled down for a landing next to the fuel bladders. With her main rotor still turning, two of Red's men quickly grabbed the fuel nozzles and refueled the thirsty chopper. Once he was topped off, Gunner eased his ship up into a ground hover and taxied over to the other side of the strip before shutting down.

By this time, Red's crew had erected the big tents that would serve as the jump CP for Buzz and the headquarter's staff. Mom and her commo people were already in operation and had established a link back to the Denver headquarters. Now that the storm had passed, she could finally get the Sky Spy satellites into operation to help with the search. Over twenty-four hours had passed since Wolff and Mojo had gone down, and time was running out.

Gunner and Legs walked into the big tent and made a beeline for the big radiant heater in front of Mom's commo console.

"You got anything on the crash site yet?" Gunner asked the operations chief.

"No," Mom shook her head. "Nothing yet. It's going to be another half hour before I get the first of the satellite feed and another fifteen minutes before we can go over it."

"We've got to get our asses in gear," Gunner said. "Those guys've been out there a long time."

Mom locked her eyes on the pilot. "Officer Jennings," her raspy voice cut like a whip. "You just make damned good and certain that you're doing your job and leave me to take care of mine. You got that?"

Gunner stiffened. "I didn't mean anything, Mom, I'm just a little . . ."

"That's Sergeant Jenkins to you, Officer," Mom snapped back. "And I want your ass out of my office right now!"

Gunner shrugged and turned around. As Sandra turned to follow him, she saw Mom give her a wink. Sandra smiled faintly as she hurried after her pilot. Sometimes Gunner forgot who was actually running the show around Dragon Flight. But what the hell, sometimes even Buzz forgot.

Chapter Nine

Deep Inside Medicine Mountain; 24 December

As soon as the door slammed shut behind them and he heard the lock click into place, Wolff knelt beside Mugabe's litter. Grabbing him by his good shoulder, he shook him awake. "Mojo! Wake up! Wake up!"

The gunner slowly opened his eyes. "Where are we?" he asked weakly.

"You're not going to believe this, but we're inside a fucking mountain."

"You're right," Mojo said as he slowly sat up and looked around the small room. "I *don't* believe it. What is this, the set for the next James Bond movie?"

"I don't know fuck all," Wolff shook his head. "I couldn't get any information out of the guys who brought us here. All I know is that this is definitely some kind of heavy-duty operation."

"How long was I out of it?" Mojo asked, wincing as he reached up to check his arm.

"A day and a half. I got you to an abandoned cabin and had gone back outside to cut firewood when a bunch of maggots with guns showed up and brought us here."

"What the hell's going on here?" Mojo asked. "Why would they want to hold us prisoner?"

69

"I don't know," Wolff answered, leaning closer and turning his eyes from side to side as he shrugged his shoulders slightly in an attempt to communicate that they might be under observation.

"I explained to them that we were Tac Force and we were on a winter training flight when our ship quit running on us, but they wouldn't talk to me."

Mojo swung his legs down over the side of the litter. "What're we going to do now?"

"Beats me," Wolff shrugged. "But I've got a real bad feeling that we're going to be here for quite some time."

There was a rattling noise on the other side of the door and it suddenly slammed open. The man with the pistol appeared in the doorway. He was wearing a blue coverall uniform now, but the pistol was still strapped to his waist. "You," he said pointing to Wolff. "Come with me."

Wolff slowly got to his feet. "What about my partner?" He pointed to Mojo.

"He stays here for now."

"Go on," Mugabe said. "I'll be okay."

"You sure?" Wolff looked worried.

Mugabe nodded. "Go."

As Wolff stepped out into the hall, two guards armed with submachine guns fell in behind him. The man with the pistol led him down the hall and opened a door onto what looked like a security guard office. A big man with shaggy red hair and a bushy beard got up from behind a bank of TV monitors and turned to face him as he walked into the room.

"Rick Wolff," the pilot said, walking up with his right hand out.

The man ignored his hand. "You two are chopper cops, right?"

Wolff lowered his hand. "Yes, we're with the Tac Force unit in Denver."

The big man studied him for a moment. "Where did your chopper go down?"

"I don't really have any idea," Wolff admitted. "We were flying along on our way to Cheyenne when the power cut off and we . . ."

The big man suddenly stepped up to him and slammed his fist into the pit of Wolff's stomach. The pilot was caught off guard and the blow drove him to his knees. He gasped with pain as he stood up.

"Shut the fuck up and answer the question. What were you two doing flying over this place?"

"I told you," Wolff panted. "We . . ."

"The man on the TV news says that you two were up here snooping around," the big man interrupted him. "Looking for downed aircraft."

"We were doing that," Wolff admitted, "but we were on our way over to Cheyenne."

"Why do you think them planes went down?"

"We don't know," Wolff shrugged. "That's what we were looking for."

"What did you find out?" the big man sneered.

"Nothing," Wolff said slowly, "but I've got an idea that you might know something about it."

The big man threw his head back and laughed. "You're pretty smart for a fucking cop. You're right, but you're not going to be able to do anything about it now, are you?"

Wolff said nothing.

"For the moment," the big man explained, "you're going to sit right where you are, but in a couple of days, you're going back out in the snow."

The big man caught the look on Wolff's face and laughed. "You're going back out all right, but we're going to see to it that you kind of get frozen in the process." He grinned broadly. "We want to leave something behind for your friends to find."

"Why are you doing this?" Wolff asked. "We don't even know where we are."

The big man leaned closer to the pilot. "The only reason you're still alive is because the boss wants it that way. If it

71

had been up to me, I'd have had my boys kill you back at the cabin. As it is, though, the boss told me to wait until after the operation is over, so don't get your hopes up. It's just a stay of execution, as you cops call it."

Wolff said nothing.

"Two more of you guys roughed up one of my men pretty badly last night and threw him in jail. Broke his leg, I understand, so I'm looking forward to watching you two bastards freeze to death."

"I don't know anything about that," Wolff said. "We were lost in the woods last night."

"When we get done with you," the man said softly, "you're going to wish you'd stayed in those fucking woods."

"Do you have a doctor or a medic in here?" Wolff asked. "My partner was hurt in the crash and he needs medical attention."

The big man frowned before breaking out in laughter. "You've got to be kidding me. You want me patch up a cop?!"

"You want to watch us freeze to death, don't you?" Wolff asked sarcastically. "If you're going to do that, my partner has to stay alive."

The man stopped laughing. "You got a point there. I don't want either one of you two assholes dying on me too soon. I'll send someone in to look at him. And I'll tell you what, we'll even feed you."

He laughed again. "Yep, I want to keep you two boys alive for a little while yet." He turned to one of the guards. "Take 'em back to the room."

Mojo was sitting up when the guards shoved Wolff back into the cell. "What'd you find out?"

"We've got us a real problem here," Wolff reported. "There's a mountain man in here who says that he's going to throw us out in the snow to freeze to death."

"What!"

"Yeah," Wolff said softly. "And I think I just found out

who's responsible for all those planes going down."

"Oh shit!"

"Captain!" Mom's voice was urgent. "You'd better come over here."

"What you got?"

"I just got a call from One Three. He's over the Forest Service access road and he says that there's a huge convoy of civilian vehicles headed our way. He says that they're packed with people carrying signs."

Buzz frowned. "What kind of signs?"

Mom shrugged. "As near as he can tell, it's the Clean Earth party."

"For Christ's sake!" Buzz exploded. "What the hell do they think they're going to do up here? Why aren't they doing something useful, like picketing Exxon?"

"Maybe they're going to try to picket us?"

"In a pig's ass," Buzz shorted. "Tell Zoomie to get in here."

The Tac Platoon leader entered the CP tent on the run. "You wanted me, sir?"

"We've got a convoy of protesters on the way up here," Buzz said. "I want you to get your boys suited up for crowd control and keep those people the hell out of the way of our operation."

"Protesters, sir?"

Buzz smiled thinly. "Environmentalists, the Clean Earth party."

"No problem, sir," Zoomie grinned. "I'm on the way."

The TacPlatoon men were just finishing putting up their tent when Zoomie raced up. "We've got protestors on the way," he said. "Get into full riot gear and stand by for crowd control."

"Sergeant Garcia," Zoomie turned to his second in command. "I'll take half of the platoon myself and I want you to mount the rest on snowmobiles and stand by as a mobile reserve."

73

Garcia grinned. "Can do."

"Get 'em moving, we only have a few minutes."

Ten minutes later, Jack Zumwald stood in the middle of the airstrip at the head of a line of ten Tac cops in black riot gear. The men wore their full Kevlar armor with face shields, just in case things got serious, but they were only armed with riot control weapons: batons, gas grenade launchers, and shotguns. The serious weaponry was with Sergeant Garcia and the reserve section.

At the far end of the airstrip, the Clean Earthers got out of their pickups and four-wheel-drive rigs and lined up with their signs. When Zoomie noticed that several of them were wearing gas masks, he slowly smiled and activated his internal platoon radio.

"Okay, boys," he said. "Listen up. We've got at least thirty people out there, and some of them are smart asses wearing gas masks, so it looks like they intend to get serious. Grenadiers, load up the sting gas and the ring grenades. When I give the word, hit 'em hard and break 'em up fast. I don't want them to get anywhere near the choppers or the rest of our command post."

A chorus of enthusiastic catcalls and yells answered his announcement. All cops hate crowd-control work, and Zoomie's men were no exception. But they had learned that the best way to deal with that kind of situation was to get the mob under control as quickly as possible.

Behind the police line, one of the Griffins revved up its turbines and lifted off the snow-covered airfield. Climbing to a hundred feet, it took up a position over the heads of the protestors. Several of them looked up and shook their signs at the circling chopper.

Standing outside the door of the mobile CP tent, Buzz watched as the protestors started down the airstrip in a line. He raised his portable radio to his lips.

"Dragon One Two, Command One," he radioed to the Griffin hovering over their heads. "Read 'em the Riot Act."

"This is the Tactical Police Force," the pilot's voice

boomed from the external speakers mounted on the helicopter. "You are trespassing on Federal property. Be advised that the Tactical Police Act has been invoked. You are required to obey the orders of the Tactical Police and leave Federal property immediately. Failure to do so will result in your being arrested under the provisions of the act."

For a moment there was silence on the airstrip, then a chant rose from the protestors. "TPF go away! Leave the woods on Christmas Day!"

Zoomie grinned and keyed his throat mike. "Piece of cake, guys. They don't even know what day it is."

Buzz stood with his jaws locked and counted off the seconds. When a minute had passed and there was no sign that the protestors were going to leave, he keyed the radio. "Tac One, this is Command One. Clear the airstrip. Take everyone into custody and secure them for transport out of here. How copy?"

Zoomie's face broke out in a broad smile. "Tac One, good copy." He switched over to his platoon frequency. "Okay, boys, let's do it. Move out."

The line of Tac cops snapped their face visors down and started for the end of the airstrip at a slow, measured march, their weapons held at port arms.

Zoomie caught a glimpse of someone at the edge of the crowd taping the action with a video camera. "Command One, Tac One," he called back to the CP. "They've got a camera crew filming this."

"This is Command One," Buzz ordered. "Pull his plug."

"Tac One, copy."

Zumwald quickly radioed to Garcia with the reserve, and two snowmobiles broke away and raced for the cameraman. The man tried to run, but the snowmobiles easily caught up with him and cut him off. The Tac cops confiscated the video camera and, after cuffing the cameraman, put him in the back of one of the machines.

The protestors screamed at the men on the snowmobiles and angrily waved their signs. "TPF go away! Leave the woods on Christmas Day!"

The protestors broke into a run for the CP. Zoomie's men halted and braced for the assault. Some unenlightened soul made the mistake of throwing a snowball with a rock inside of it at Zoomie's men. It hit the cop in the neck and he cried out. More snowballs followed.

This was what Zoomie had been waiting for. "Grenadiers," he snapped. "Give 'em the gas."

Four Tac cops raised their grenade launchers to their shoulders and fired. The 40mm CN gas grenades flew through the air and landed in front of the protestors. A second barrage was aimed to land behind them. In seconds, the mob was covered with a cloud of persistent, crystalline tear gas.

The chants immediately turned to cries as the gas produced its desired effect. Unlike nonpersistent tear gas, these gas crystals clung to clothing, skin, and hair, producing a burning as well as the usual eye irritation and choking sensations. An untrained person could tough out a cloud of non-persistent gas, but this stuff was different. Rubbing the eyes only made the effects of the gas worse, and often made the eyelids swell shut. Also, since the gas crystals got into the lungs, they caused a temporary choking sensation that made the person gasp for air and left him unable to think about anything else except breathing.

Most of the protestors immediately went down on their hands and knees in the snow, weeping and fighting for air, but the few in gas masks ripped the signs off the clubs they carried and charged the police line.

"Take 'em out!" Zoomie ordered as his men braced to take the charge.

The grenadiers quickly changed the magazines in their launchers to ring grenades and fired point blank at the charging protestors. Ring grenades were better than conventional rubber bullets for stopping a man. Made from hard rubber and shaped like tubular airfoils, the ring grenades spun upon leaving the launcher. This spinning stabilized their flight, enabling them to be aimed as accurately as rifle bullets. When they hit a man, they stopped him in his tracks without causing any permanent damage.

In seconds, all of these protestors were on their hands and knees too, downed by the ring grenades. The protest was over.

Zoomie clicked in his throat mike. "Okay, boys," he radioed. "Cuff 'em and move 'em out."

Chapter Ten

It was a pitiful looking mob of would-be protestors who huddled in the back of the mess hall tent on the edge of the airstrip. Their colorful ski jackets and pants were covered with mud, their hands were cuffed behind their backs with plastic restraints. Tears still flowed from their gas-stung eyes, and several of them were nursing bruises from the rubber ring grenades. Even the ones who had not been hurt looked scared half to death. Usually, protesting was great fun, it got them a lot of attention from the media and made them feel that they were important and were calling the shots. What had gone wrong this time?

They'd had a lot of fun protesting for years. For them, protesting had become more of a social event than a way to make a statement. It was a great way to make friends and connections, "networking," as they called it, but none of them had ever come up against the Tac Force before. And until today's abortive protest, they had not learned the simple lesson that so many criminals across the country had learned the hard way: Do not fuck with the Tac Force.

These people were so accustomed to breaking any law they wanted in the name of their various causes, and getting away with it, that they had forgotten that they lived in a nation of laws, not causes. They had broken the law frequently and had never been called to account for it. Therefore they had come to believe that they were exempt from the rules that governed the behavior of the average American citizen.

They saw themselves as a privileged elite. They were all very well aware that they had civil rights, but they had never tried to do their little civil disobedience number in front of the United States Tactical Police Force before. The Tac Force had just taught them that their civil rights went hand in hand with equal civil responsibilities. And as they had just been taught, one of those civil responsibilities was to obey the law.

In the future, most of these protestors would be very careful when and where they tried to disrupt society. And if the Tac Force ever told them to get lost again, they would listen.

Most of them would . . . There were still a few diehards who always thought that God was on their side, whatever side that was, laws or not.

One of the environmentalists struggled awkwardly to his feet, his hands cuffed behind his back with plastic restraints. "I demand to speak to your commander immediately," he said to the Tac Platoon cop who had strolled over to tell him to sit back down.

The cop smiled. "Demand in one hand and shit in the other, pal. See which gets full the fastest."

"I have my rights!"

"The only right you have on Federal property, mister," the cop answered patiently, "is the right to do exactly *what* you're told, *when* you're told to do it. Didn't they explain that to you in civics class?"

"But you were raping the earth!"

The Tac cop walked up to the protestor and leaned close to his face. "For your information, asshole," he said softly, "we are out here looking for a downed aircraft with two of our men onboard it."

"But you are polluting the forest with your machines." The man felt his face get red.

"At least we weren't polluting it with bullshit," the cop smiled. "And if you're so concerned about saving trees, why are your signs made out of paper?"

The environmentalist frowned. "But they're made from recycled paper."

"Recycled or not, paper still comes from trees. Now sit down and shut up."

The environmentalist sat back down.

Zoomie came into the CP tent to report on the results of his operation. "We've got thirty-one suspects in custody," he read from his notebook. "And there's not a single piece of ID on any of them. No driver's licenses, no Social Security cards, student body cards, Unicards. *Nada.*"

Buzz smiled. The old "no ID" trick was designed to make booking protestors more difficult for the police. It might cause a local police force a little trouble, but it was no problem for the Tac Force. The Federal Detention Center in Denver had lots of empty beds, and he didn't care if it took weeks for these assholes to be identified and turned loose on bail.

"No sweat," Buzz said, grinning from ear to ear. "Book 'em all on John and Jane Doe warrants as suspected illegal aliens. Alert the Immigration people and make sure that they run them through the full treatment."

Zoomie smiled broadly too. The Immigration Service would have fun with this lot, and the next time they planned to get themselves arrested, they would make sure that they had their IDs with them.

"And, when we know who they are," Buzz continued, "run a full Wants and Warrants — Federal, state, and local — on all of them, men and women alike," he shrugged. "Who knows what we'll turn up."

He paused for a moment. "Also, when that's done, run them through the IRS as well. We might find that some of them have been cheating on their taxes or are not repaying their student loans."

"Be glad to, sir," Zoomie smiled.

"Assholes," Buzz muttered.

"Buzz," Mom called out from her console at the other side of the room. "We've got some VIP on the line who wants to talk to you."

"Who is it?"

"A Benton Sloan. That guy who's running for president on the Clean Earth ticket. He's calling from his campaign headquarters in Las Vegas."

Buzz closed his eyes for a moment and took a deep breath. "What in the hell does he want?"

Mom shrugged. "He says that you are violating the civil rights of his people and he wants you to release them immediately."

"Does he now?" Buzz grinned as he quickly strode across the tent. "Let me talk to him."

Mom handed him the phone. "Mr. Sloan, this is Captain J.D. Corcran of the United States Tactical Police Force, what can I do for you?"

"Captain," came the firm voice on the other end of the line. "I understand that your men have arrested peaceful protestors and . . ."

"You understand wrong," Buzz interrupted him. "I have arrested people on Federal property who are in violation of the provisions of the Federal Tactical Police Act."

"But," Sloan said firmly, "my information is that they were protesting peacefully."

"Your information is wrong," Buzz cut in. "They refused to obey my orders to disperse and they assaulted my officers. Both of which are Federal crimes under the Tac Force Act, and they will be charged with those crimes."

"But they're just kids who are trying to save the earth!" Sloan said.

"If they're old enough to do the crime, they're old enough to face charges."

"But you can't arrest them!"

"I just did."

Buzz put the phone down. "Presidential candidate or not," he told Mom, "I won't take any more calls from that guy. If he calls back, you can tell him I said that if he wants to get these people back, he can go down and pay their bail at the Federal Detention Center in Denver."

"Washington may not like that, sir," Mom reminded him. "He is a candidate and this is an election year."

"I don't give a shit what some politician likes or dislikes," Buzz restated a well-known fact about himself. "Those assholes broke the law and they will be treated like any other criminals. Now, see how fast you can get one of our C-9s back here so we can get these people out of my operating area."

"Yes, sir."

Back at his headquarters in Las Vegas, Buck Sloan sat and stared out the window of his penthouse office. Damn those cops, anyway! He pushed the button on the intercom to the outer office. Mattiese answered immediately. "Yes, sir."

"Come in here," Sloan said. "We have to get out a news release about those demonstrators."

Mattiese hurried in and sat down, a pad of paper and a pen in his hands. Sloan leaned back in his chair and folded his hands behind his head. "Have you found out how many of our people were arrested?"

Mattiese consulted his notes. "Apparently some thirty-one of them. Twelve men and nineteen women."

"Good," Sloan answered. "How many were injured?"

"I don't have a count on that yet."

"As soon as you get those figures, put out something deploring the brutality of the Tac Force in putting down a peaceful demonstration on the eve of the birthday of the Prince of Peace."

Mattiese winced. He hated tying religion in with politics any more than he absolutely had to.

"Try to get some shots of the wounded kids. Christmas Eve massacre, that sort of thing."

"What about our concern for the missing cops from that crash?"

"Play that up too, but say that our concern for them, and their families if they have any, does not justify beating up on peaceful protestors. Do the 'God's on our side' kind of thing and hit the Christmas angle real hard. You know what I mean, young adults concerned about the future of the earth at this particular time of the year."

Mattiese winced inwardly. Maybe when this campaign was over he'd finally look for an honest job. "I'll get it out this afternoon."

"Next," Sloan said, "I need the number of that senator who's on the National Parks Commission."

"What do you want with him?" Mattiese frowned.

Sloan smiled. "I think he can help us get a little better coverage for our demonstration," he said. *And get those fucking cops out of there before they stumble onto something,* he thought. Specifically, before they stumble onto something that could hold up the New Dawn project. For it to have the maximum effect, it had to go off on time.

"I'll get that for you, Buck," Mattiese said as he got to his feet.

Now that that little problem was taken care of, Sloan turned his mind to a much more serious problem, the fact that one of his security force at the facility had gotten his sorry ass arrested and thrown in the Federal slam.

He had done everything he could to impress on those

wildmen of Bowman's that they had to maintain a low profile, but every time they went to Grimsley to get drunk and laid, something like this always seemed to happen. Usually the fact that the town's sheriff was on his payroll was enough to keep the situation under control, but this time it had gotten completely out of hand, and this Sunderland asshole was in the hands of the Tac Force.

He'd had serious reservations from the first about trusting the security of his operation to a bunch of half-wild mountain men and Hell's Angels rejects, but his backers had insisted that he use them. That was the problem when you were dealing with the Mob: they had a unique concept about who was and was not to be trusted.

Sloan had proposed that he hire mercenaries, highly trained and disciplined professionals, for his security force. But his backers had vetoed that idea. Instead, they wanted him to use some of their old drug army contacts—ex-bikers, mountain men, and outlaws. And since they were the ones who had made the whole program possible, he'd had no choice but to let them have their way.

Now one of these assholes had assaulted a chopper cop. And worse than that, the cop he had assaulted was from the same unit that was looking for the crew of the downed Griffin chopper. If anyone got the bright idea to investigate this guy's background thoroughly, or if Sunderland thought that he could cut a deal with the Feds and spill his guts for a lighter sentence, they'd all be in a world of shit. But since the Family had forced this guy on him, as far as Sloan was concerned, they could take care of him as well.

He smiled as he picked up the phone and activated his satellite link, placing a call to New Jersey. Back at his facility under the mountain, his technicians would be able to intercept his phone call and unscramble it, but since they were all working for him, it really didn't matter if they overheard him or not.

In fact, maybe it would be good for discipline if the word

got out that Sunderland was going to get iced for not keeping his mouth shut. Particularly if he got iced in the right manner.

Sloan smiled. He was confident that the Family's enforcers would know how to deal with a snitch. Even a snitch in a Federal lockup.

Chapter Eleven

The Forest Service AirStrip; 24 December

Now that Buzz had the mountain airstrip all to himself, it was time to launch the Griffins and get started again on the search for Wolff and Mugabe's chopper.

Mom had still not been able to get any information on the crash site from the Sky Spy satellites, but now that Zoomie's men were warmed up from their morning's exercise, they could be broken up into two-man search teams with a snowmobile carried in the back of each of the three Griffins. Each chopper would fly a search pattern in the vicinity of Wolff's last radar plot, their sensors and eyeballs turned up all the way. If they found anything that looked interesting, they could set down, offload the snowmobile, and conduct a ground search. It was a long shot, but it was all that they had to go on for now.

Buzz's aircrew briefing was short and to the point. They had already lost too much valuable time today and Buzz didn't want to waste any more. "Listen up," he said, quieting the low rumble of conversation. "I'm going to make this fast. Take out your maps and note this location."

He tapped a point on the large map next to him. "This is the place where the last radar plot shows that they were. I want all of you to use this location as the start point for the search."

"I have divided the area around this point into three

search sectors, Alpha, Bravo and Charlie. One Four has Alpha, One Two has Bravo and One Three has Charlie. Until further notice, One Four will take over as Dragon Lead and will coordinate the search. Watch your fuel carefully and watch what you're doing, I don't want to have to go looking for anyone else. Also, stay in constant communication with Dragon Control."

Buzz looked round the tent. "Are there any questions?"

There were none.

"All right, people," Buzz sounded like a football coach in the final quarter of the Super Bowl. "Get out there and find those guys."

The air crews quickly filed out of the tent and ran for their choppers. Zoomie and one of his sergeants climbed into the back of Dragon One Four, Gunner and Leg's machine, joining the snowmobile and the paramedic who were already waiting for them.

After checking the snowmobile's tiedowns, Zoomie put the spare flight helmet on and checked in with Gunner. "We're ready back here," he said. "Let's do it."

Up in the cockpit, Gunner and Sandra quickly ran through the checklist and fired up the turbines. The cold mountain air filled with the warm smell of burning kerosene as the Griffin's rotors came up to speed. A second later, Gunner called for permission to take off. Mom came back with clearance and he twisted the throttle, bringing One Four up into a low hover to taxi out to the runway. A second later, the turbines screamed as he opened them up and headed down the strip in a gunship takeoff.

As soon as Gunner lifted off and banked away to the north, Zoomie settled down for what promised to be a long, but he hoped not boring, day in the air.

Zumwald was never bored when there was even the faintest possibility of going into action. Zoomie was the consummate adrenaline junkie, and action was the reason why he had joined the Tac Force in the first place. Mountain climbing, skydiving and bungee cord jumping just hadn't been exciting enough for him. Like any addict, he had craved bigger and better highs, and that was exactly what commanding Dragon Flight's Tac Platoon had given him. As the leader of the hard-hitting ground combat arm of the TPF, he had found enough excitement to fulfill his craving for putting his life on the line.

Even on a mission like this, where he faced long hours in the air searching a frozen wilderness with almost no chance of getting into a firefight, there was still the remote possibility he would find himself in danger. Maybe he would come upon a hungry grizzly bear or something like that to make it interesting, and that was enough for him.

He looked out the window at the snow-covered mountains and forests below. He had really gotten off on his winter tactical training in the Rockies, and this was the first time he'd had a chance to put that training into practice. He probably wouldn't get into a firefight down there, but he would still have to fight Old Man Winter, and that wasn't going to be easy. It was good that it wouldn't be easy, because that would be boring, and Zoomie Zumwald hated to be bored.

"We're coming up on the start point," Sandra announced to Zoomie over the intercom. "Wake up back there and start looking out the windows."

Zoomie turned around in his seat so he could see out his side of the chopper and keyed the helmet mike. "We're ready back here."

Gunner banked his machine over and started flying the search pattern. To both the right and the left of him, the other two Griffins did the same.

In the left-hand seat of Dragon One Four, Sandra bent over her sensor readouts, trying to make sense out of the meager data she was getting from her search. For this sweep she had everything turned on full blast; the infrared detector, the Doppler radar, the mass proximeter, the terrain-mapping system, everything. But regardless of the sophistication built into the Griffin's sensor equipment, she wasn't getting anything that she could use.

She had, however, sent Gunner down lower to check out a couple of grazing deer who had triggered the IR, and they had chased a bear who had showed up on the Doppler radar, but she wasn't picking up anything that indicated a crashed aircraft anywhere below them.

Part of the problem was that everything was covered by several feet of snow. To the IR sensor, everything showed up as having the same temperature, below freezing. The drifted snow blurred the outlines of the land and the mapping radar showed only the gently curving surface of the snow banks. She knew that the shattered remains of a Griffin chopper were somewhere below them buried under the snow, but she was damned if she could find it.

All three choppers were tac linked together, and Sandra's computer map showing the area they had covered was growing bigger and bigger with every passing minute. They were covering every inch of the ground, but they weren't finding anything.

In the back of the chopper, Zoomie was going snow-blind squinting against the glare of the drifted snow below them. He blinked to wipe away a tear and jerked his eyes back down. There, in the middle of that stand of timber, he caught a flash of something out of place. He clicked in the intercom.

"Gunner," he called up to the pilot. "Bank around to the right and come down a little lower over those trees, I thought I saw something."

"Copy," Gunner called back as he put the Griffin into a turn to go back over the forest.

"There!" Zoomie shouted. "See it? The tops of the trees are cut off!"

"I see it!" Gunner called back.

"That's where they went down!" Zoomie shouted, reaching for the snowmobile tiedowns. "Find a place to set this

89

sucker down fast!"

Gunner quickly brought the Griffin in for a landing at the edge of the stand of timber. As Wolff had discovered, there were damned few clearings in the area large enough to set a Griffin down in. This one was just large enough to clear the tips of the forty-foot main rotor. Once he saw how dense the trees actually were, Zoomie decided against trying to use the snowmobile, so he, the sergeant, and the paramedic quickly put on their snowshoes.

As soon as they were out the door, Gunner carefully lifted out of the clearing and flew above them to guide them in the right direction. Since their personal locator beacons were operating, Sandra could track them through the thick forest without actually being able to see them under the trees.

"Tac One," she radioed. "You're approaching the last tree that shows damage. Take a heading of one three five and they should be along that line."

"Tac One, copy," Zoomie radioed. "I'm standing at the base of that tree and I can see where they came through the treetops. Right up ahead there's a mound of snow against the side of a big tree, and it's big enough to be covering a Griffin, or at least part of one. I'm going there now."

"One Four X-Ray, copy."

Zoomie ploughed his way through the waist-deep drifts to reach the edge of the mound. Brushing away the snow, he uncovered a metal surface wearing the dark blue paint of the Tac Force Griffins.

"Over here!" he shouted to his sergeant. "I think I've found it."

It took several minutes before the two men could clear away enough of the snow to see that the Griffin's fuselage section was lying on its left side. The tail boom was snapped off, and the nose was crushed, but the cockpit seemed to be okay. Opening the right-hand door, he looked in to find the ship empty.

"Fuck!"

90

"Dragon One Four, Tac One," Zumwald radioed, his breath steaming in the cold air. "We have located the wreckage, but there's no one here. The ship's totally destroyed, but the cockpit section is fairly intact. There's no blood, however, so it looks like they walked away from the crash."

"One Four, copy," Gunner answered. "Can you see which way they went?"

"Tac One, that's a negative. It's snowed heavily since they crashed, and there's just no way of telling where they've gone."

"Copy, check the wreckage to see if they took their survival pack with them."

"Wait one."

Zumwald was back on the air in seconds. "It's gone," he radioed. "And it also looks like they took the first aid kit with them as well. Maybe one of them was hurt after all."

Gunner was silent for a moment. "Copy. Fan out and start looking for them while I get back to Command One."

"Tac One, copy."

Buzz was grim faced when he handed the microphone back to Mom. "Why in the hell did they leave that chopper?" he asked, thinking out loud.

Mom shook her head and answered for him. "I don't know, but they must have had a damned good reason. They know that they're always supposed to stay at the crash site if they go down."

"Damn it, anyway," Buzz exploded. "We're back to square one again."

"But at least there's a chance that they're still alive somewhere," Mom pointed out. "We haven't found their bodies yet."

"There is that," Buzz agreed as he reached for the microphone again.

* * *

91

The Griffins started returning to the airstrip at sundown. One by one they flew in like hawks returning to the roost, circled the runway, and set down next to the fuel bladders to have their tanks topped off again. Once refueled, they rose off the ground in a low hover and taxied over to the other side of the strip and shut down for the night. As soon as the main rotors were tied down, the tired aircrews walked over to the mess tent for dinner.

The mess hall personnel had tried to create a home-away-from-home holiday air by putting out a nice buffet with all the traditional Christmas Eve foods. It was a nice meal, but it was not enough to dispel the air of gloom and disappointment that had swept across the base. Finding Wolff's chopper empty had been a blow to everyone.

Too tired to eat, Gunner and Legs picked at the food on their trays. The rest of the day had been a complete bust. When Zoomie had found the Griffin empty, Gunner had shifted the search areas to center on the wreckage, but nothing further had turned up—not so much as a single footprint or survival ration wrapper.

"I'm going back out there tonight," Gunner stated flatly as he pushed his tray away.

"Do you think Buzz will okay it?" Sandra asked.

Gunner shrugged "I don't know, but I'm going to ask him. All he can say is no." He slowly got to his feet. "You with me?"

"Sure." She pushed back her chair and stood up. "Let's do it."

The two flyers found Buzz in the communications tent going over the search reports. "Can we have a word with you, sir?" Gunner asked.

"What's up?"

"How about letting Legs and me go up again tonight, sir?" Gunner asked. "We can use the searchlight, and since its colder now, the IR sensor will pick up heat sources even better. Maybe we can pick up a campfire."

Buzz thought for a moment. It was probably a complete

waste of time and JP-4, but on the other hand it wouldn't hurt anything and the taxpayers would foot the bill for the jet fuel. "Go for it," he said.

"We'll be airborne in a few minutes," Gunner said.

"I'll put One Two on ramp alert if you find anything and need a backup."

"Thanks, sir," Sandra said, zipping up her parka.

"Don't thank me," Buzz said gruffly. "Just find those guys."

A few moments later, the beating sound of a Griffin's rotors cut through the cold night air and quickly faded into the distance.

As Gunner and Sandra flew low over the snow-covered forest, the radio played songs about peace on earth, good will to all men. Somehow, hearing that message of peace didn't make Sandra feel any better. She knew that Wolff and Mojo were not having a peaceful Christmas Eve.

Chapter Twelve

Buck Sloan was spending Christmas morning blissfully alone. Since the announcement of his candidacy, he had been lucky to spend even a single waking hour by himself. It was true that he had an early afternoon reception today and a dinner party later in the evening. But for the time being he was alone, completely alone. He had even been able to chase Mattiese away from his desk in the outer office for a few hours.

Rather than relaxing, however, Sloan was using his precious solitude to try to figure out what he was going to do about the Tac Force. He was extremely uncomfortable having them running around in the woods so close to his hidden mountain facility. Since the arrest of the demonstrators yesterday, there was still a hard-core group protesting at the entrance to the national forest, but they would be of no help. They were under strict orders not to set foot on Federal land, and since the Tac Force was flying in and out of the remote site anyway, there was nothing they could do to impede the search.

Now for the first time, Sloan fervently wished that Bowman, his security chief, had been a little less quick on the trigger of the EMP weapon. If the TPF Griffin had not been shot down, none of this would be happening. It was a little too late to worry about that now, however. Bowman had only been following his orders. Those orders had been to protect the facility at all costs.

As Sloan knew well, those orders had come not from himself but from his East Coast backers. Sure, Sloan wanted his facility air-tight, but they were the ones who were paranoid about losing the return on their investment in Sloan's facility. They had put up over a billion dollars in bribes and construction costs to make this thing work. And while the interception of secret corporate satellite communications information was paying them big dividends in the stock market, they wanted to see much more than that for their time and money.

Not only was New Dawn going to put Buck Sloan in the White House, it was also conveniently going to remove a portion of California that just happened to be the operating base of the Family's main business rivals in the area. And to the Family, that was even more important than having their man elected. That was the real return they were expecting on their investment. Their successful entry into the Sun Belt required that the competition be eliminated.

Sloan was worried about their investment too. He knew that if this plan didn't pay off as he had promised he might still get elected to the White House, but he would become the first American president to be assassinated in the new millennium. There was no doubt in his mind about that. And right now, the only thing standing in the way of his plans was the TPF.

He briefly entertained the thought of asking his backers to see if they could put some political pressure on the Tac Force to pull those guys out of the woods and send them back to chasing petty drug dealers. But even though they owned enough politicians to form a congressional quorum, that would be difficult. Unlike all too many of the traditional police forces, the Tac Force had proved that they could neither be bought nor bribed.

The congressional watchdog committee that oversaw the Tac Force operations could be bought, and was all the time, but they had almost no influence on what the Tac cops actually did while they were doing it. All the committee could do was to hold endless hearings on past Tac Force operations while the committee members preened and postured on camera for the folks back home.

Sloan swore to himself that one of the first things he would do after he took over the Oval Office would be to completely disband the United States Tactical Police Force. Moreover, he knew that he would probably have more than enough support in Congress to do it. Like the Mob, most congressmen were uncomfortable when they had to deal with men who could not be bought. And one of the examples he would use to good effect against the Tac Force was the arrest and detention of those dumbass kids at the Forest Service airstrip. The media was starting to call them the "Christmas Demonstrators" and was already making martyrs of them. That would fit right into his plans.

He thought about trying one more time to apply pressure on the Tac Force through the Department of the Interior by hammering hard on the environmental damage they were doing to the forest. But the one congressman on the National Parks Commission that Sloan had in his pocket had been of no help at all. It looked like he was just going to have to hold tight and hope that the chopper cops didn't get too close to the mountain itself.

The other pressing question on his mind was what he should do about those two cops from the downed chopper. This was the first time that anyone had survived an aircraft downing by his EMP weapon. So far, when the search parties found the wreckage, everyone on board was dead. It was neat and tidy that way, but these two guys had somehow been able to bring their chopper in for a semicontrolled crash landing. And the strength built into their Griffin had allowed them to survive the crash.

He still planned to dump them back out in the cold and let them to freeze to death. If it was done right, that would be the end of it. But he also knew that it would be difficult to do it right, so he had decided to put it off for a week or so. There were bound to be tracks leading to and from the body dump site, tracks that would only invite further investigation. And that was the last thing he needed right now, more chopper cops running around in the woods.

He realized that it made more sense to just keep them locked up till after New Dawn and then send them out to die. After New Dawn, no one would have the time to be concerned about a couple of missing cops whose bodies had been found in the woods.

At least he wouldn't have to worry about that asshole Sunderland shooting off his mouth anymore; his backers had promised him that he would be taken care of tonight. The Family had people everywhere, even in the Federal Detention Center at Denver.

He checked his watch and saw that he had a couple of hours left until he was expected at the luncheon. There was still time for him to check in with his service and see how the SOLCO stock had fared before the Christmas market closing. He had to make sure that he and his company were poised and ready to exploit the confusion that would follow New Dawn. It would be the chance of a lifetime to make a killing on the market, but things would happen quickly and he would have to be ready for it.

He activated his computer and noted with pleasure that SOLCO's stock had risen more than ten points since he had announced his candidacy. Not bad, not bad at all. He checked his personal holdings and discovered that he had not been able to buy back as many shares of SOLCO as he had wanted, but with the stock's sudden rise in price, he wasn't really surprised. After doing a quick run-up of his net worth, he shut the monitor down and leaned back in his chair.

Everything was in place. All he had to do now was to wait until New Year's Day.

Though it was only the second day of the search, the pace had slowed somewhat at the remote Dragon Flight Command Post. Buzz had given his men and women time off to make phone calls back to their families and loved ones, and he had laid on a big mid-afternoon Christmas dinner to be served in the mess tent. Even during an emergency like this, Buzz knew that he had to give his people some time to do the traditional things on Christmas Day.

While the meal was being prepared back at the Forest Service airstrip, Gunner and Legs were still up in the air, continuing the search. While everyone in Dragon Flight was giving a hundred and ten percent to the effort to find Wolff and Mugabe, Gunner and Legs were beating themselves to death with it. When they weren't in the air, they were pouring over the maps and bugging Mom about the latest information she had received from the Sky Spy satellites.

Since their early afternoon refueling stop was scheduled to coincide with the Christmas meal, Gunner and Legs decided to refuel themselves while Red's men were looking after their chopper. Buzz stopped them as they walked into the mess tent together, but as had been the case after their morning flight, they had nothing new to report. They joined the others going through the chow line and took their trays over to an empty table to eat. Neither one of them really had much of an appetite, but the food looked good and they went through the motions anyway.

Sandra ate a little roast turkey and picked at the rest while Gunner drank coffee and ate berry pie. They had been silent throughout the meal. "Gunner," she said, "we're going up again, aren't we?"

"You bet." He reached for the thermos pitcher of coffee on the table to refill his cup. "We've got enough time to get in a couple more hours before dark."

"Good," she said. "I was afraid that this was going to be it for the day." She paused. "Let's ask Zoomie if he wants to go with us. He seems to pick up on a lot of things that I seem to miss."

Gunner looked up at the tone of Sandra's voice. She was starting to take the disappointment hard. The frustration of not finding the two men at the crash site was weighing on all of them, but she seemed to be taking it as a personal failure. He reached over and gently patted her hand. "We'll find 'em," he tried to sound reassuring. "Those two guys are too damned stubborn to die."

Sandra's eyes narrowed when she heard the word *die*. That was the part of this that no one was discussing yet. What were they going to do if they found their bodies? "They're not dead, Gunner." Her voice was hard and told him that she was not even going to discuss that possibility.

When Gunner saw that he had put his foot in his mouth he pushed back his chair and stood up. "I'll go talk to Zoomie now," he said, spotting Zumwald sitting at a nearby table in front of an empty mess hall tray. It was a gold-plated bitch to have Mojo and the Wolfman lost in the woods, but Zoomie wasn't going to let something like that get in the way of his enjoying a good meal.

Gunner walked up behind him and laid his hand on the Tac Platoon leader's shoulder. "How'd you like to get in a little flight time this afternoon, my man?"

Zumwald looked up from his empty tray. "Sure," he said with a grin. "That's just the thing to settle all this turkey and dressing. When are we leaving?"

"As soon as you can get your shit together," Gunner answered. "I've had the ground crew load one of the snowmobiles into the back of One Four and we're ready to crank her up as soon as you are."

"Well, shit," Zoomie said, pushing his chair back and getting to his feet. "Don't just stand there jacking your jaws, man, let's do it."

On his way out of the tent, Zoomie snagged another piece of pumpkin pie off the serving table and ate it on his way out to the flight line. In this kind of weather, a guy needed to keep the fires stoked.

"Since we're all on our own up here today," Gunner said, once they were in the air over the search area, "what do you say about just picking a likely place and checking it out? We can't do any worse than we've done trying to do it one square at a time. Maybe we can find some place that they might have gone for shelter."

"That's a good idea," Sandra said as she quickly called up the map on her screen. "We're sure as hell not getting anywhere with what we've been doing."

She studied her screen for a few moments and punched in a highlight to mark a terrain feature.

"It looks like there may be some kind of a structure close to the base of the mountain," she said. "It's quite a ways from the crash site, but it's the only man-made thing anywhere around here."

Gunner switched the image over to his land navigation screen and banked the Griffin around to home in on it. "Sounds good to me."

Flying low to the ground, the Griffin was over the small cabin that Wolff and Mugabe had stopped over at in less than half an hour. As it came into sight, Sandra trained all her sensors on it and studied her readouts intently, but she didn't pick up a thing. There was no Doppler, no IR, no audio. "Damn," she said. "Nothing."

Gunner flew down a little lower and circled the cabin. All he could see was that the front door was hanging open. "Let's take a look anyway," he said. "That way we can check it off the list of possibilities."

"Why not."

The pilot keyed the intercom and called back to the rear compartment. "Zoomie," he said. "We've got a cabin down here. It looks deserted and Legs can't pick up anything, but how about checking it out anyway?"

"Sure thing," he called backup. "Put me down and I'll take the snowmobile in and cover the surrounding area at the same time."

"Copy," Gunner answered as he cut back on the throttle and used the collective to feather the main rotor blades to set up for the landing. "We're going in now."

Dragon One Four flared out and settled to the ground in a flurry of snowflakes blown up by the rotor blades. Zoomie had the side door slid back and the winch hooked up to the snowmobile in under a minute.

"Okay," he called up to Gunner. "Unlock the arm."

Gunner flipped the activating switch on the control panel and the winch arm unfolded from the fuselage. Using the rear compartment winch controls, Zoomie carefully guided the snowmobile out of the rear compartment and lowered it down to the ground. He punched the cable release button and jumped down after it.

"Okay," he yelled. "Fold it up."

While Gunner retracted the winch, Zoomie cranked up the snowmobile and motored away. As soon as the machine was well out of the way of the rotor blast, Gunner lifted off again to scout ahead for him from the air.

Chapter Thirteen

The Mountain Cabin; 25 December

Zoomie's racing snowmobile crested the snowdrift and crashed down on the other side in a flurry of powder snow. He dodged around another big drift and broke into the clearing at the edge of the woods. Ahead was the small cabin that Gunner had spotted. Braking to a halt in front of it, he saw that the door hung open and a small pile of drifted snow had blown inside.

He dismounted the snowmobile, pulled his Glock pistol, and flicked the safety off. There was a new covering of light snow on the ground, but when he bent down to look closer, he thought that he could detect faint signs of traffic under the top layer.

Even though he wasn't expecting trouble, Zoomie approached the cabin cautiously, more from instinct than from real concern. He entered the door low, his weapon at the ready, but the one-room cabin was empty. Feeling a little foolish, he holstered his Glock and looked around the room. The first thing he noticed was that a big wooden table had been turned upside down and the legs were broken off. Obviously someone had been using it for firewood.

He quickly crossed over to the potbellied stove at the back end of the room and, pulling his glove off, laid his hand on the rusty side of the metal stove. It was as cold as the rest of the place, but he opened the door to the firebox anyway. The ashes inside, though, looked as if they were fresh. It was hard to tell with ashes, but they didn't have that leftover look.

He walked over to take a closer look at the upside down table. Two of the heavy wooden legs were missing and had undoubtably gone into the stove for fuel. The real question was who had burned the table legs and when had they done it? Had they been burned by Wolff and Mugabe sometime yesterday or had they been used by some cross-country skier who had stopped in to warm up sometime during the last month or so?

There was no way that he could tell what had happened here—or when it had happened. But the boys in forensic should be able to make something of it without too much difficulty. They were always bragging that they could reconstruct a crime scene from the dust in the air, so this would be a good test of their expertise.

Being careful to touch as little as he could, Zoomie made a thorough check of the entire room before he walked back outside. Pulling the personal communicator from the back of his belt, he glanced up at the Griffin circling overhead and keyed the mike to make his report.

Even though he had not found the two men, this was possibly the first solid clue they had, other than the wreckage, and it would be a nice Christmas present for the people back at the CP.

"One Four, this is Tac One."

"One Four, go ahead," Gunner answered.

"This is Tac One, it's empty," Zoomie reported. "But I think that someone's been staying here sometime in the last couple of weeks."

"Out-fucking-standing!" Gunner shouted enthusiastically. "I'll call Buzz."

"Also," Zoomie added. "Tell him we need to get the

forensic people in here ASAP."

"One Four, copy."

Zoomie glanced around. The thought crossed his mind that as long as he was here he might as well snoop around and see what else he could find. But he curbed the urge. The forensic team wouldn't like him tramping through the clues.

In the security force office of the hidden facility, Fats Bowman watched the surveillance screen as Zoomie stepped out of the cabin and made his radio call to the Griffin circling overhead. Solar-powered remote video cameras covered all of the possible approaches to Sloan's facility and were monitored twenty-four hours a day.

"I sure as hell hope your boys did a real good job of cleaning that place up, Frank," he said slowly as he watched the screen show the Griffin flaring out for a landing in front of the small shack. "If not, we're going to have those fucking Federal cops combing the whole area looking for those two assholes."

Frank Sylvan might have been on the run from the law for an outstanding drug trafficking warrant, but he was nobody's dummy. There was a good reason why the Family had made him Bowman's second in command. He had a well-deserved reputation for being smart and for paying good attention to details.

"Don't worry, Fats," he replied. "They swept it clean, just like I told them to. Believe me, I know what I'm doing. Every last trace of those cops ever having been there is long gone. I even picked up that hatchet the guy had been cutting wood with."

Bowman wasn't considered quite as smart as Sylvan, but Sloan's backers valued him because he was very good at making collections for them. He was so good, in fact, that he had been sent to the mountain hideout to stay out of sight for a couple of months after having made an example of someone who had thought that he could be late with a loan payment.

"It'd better be," he growled. "Sloan's nervous enough as it is with those fuckers flying around all over the place up here. And if there's any more fuckups, the Family's going to have *my* ass, not yours."

"It's okay, Fats," Sylvan tried to reassure him. "Believe me. They're not going to find anything that will tip them off that those guys were ever there."

"Speaking of cops," Bowman said, "how are our two guests today?"

"The white guy keeps asking for a medic to take a look at the other one."

"He asked me the same thing when we brought 'em in," Bowman said. "So maybe we'd better send Doc in to take a look at him."

"Yeah," Sylvan smiled. "We gotta keep those two alive until we can kill 'em."

Bowman laughed until the tears rolled down his fat cheeks. "That's real good, Frank, I like it. Keep 'em alive till we can ice 'em."

"I'll get Doc to look at the bastard later this afternoon," Sylvan said.

"Make sure you keep 'em covered while Doc's in there," Bowman cautioned. "I don't want them trying anything cute."

"They'll behave themselves," Sylvan promised with a grin. "Believe me."

"They'd better," Bowman said. "The boss ain't going to want to hear about any more screw-ups, and he'll be up here at the end of the week."

"What's going to happen after this New Dawn thing goes down?" Sylvan asked. "How much longer are we going to have to live like moles in this mountain? It's been three months now and I'm sick of it."

"I don't know," the big man shrugged. "I never asked him. All I know is that since Sunderland got his dumb ass picked up, we're all restricted here until it's over, but he never said anything about afterward, so I don't know how much longer he wants us to stay here."

Sylvan shuddered involuntarily. "This place's really driving me bug shit, man. I want to look up and see the sky instead of this fucking rock. I've got to get outta here before I go crazy."

"Shit, man," Bowman laughed. "I thought you already were, that's why you're here." Since he always did his best work at night, Bowman didn't miss the sky. "But don't worry, it'll be over real soon."

Muttering under his breath, Sylvan went to get the medic. Damn those cops, anyway.

Gunner's message about finding the cabin broke up the Christmas Day celebration at the airstrip. The other two flight crews and the search teams ran for their machines and were airborne in minutes. Everyone else crowded around the radios to listen in as the choppers scoured the area around the cabin, but when the Griffins came back at sundown without finding anything more, the good spirits quickly vanished again. If anything, everyone was even a little more downhearted than they had been before. This was the second time that they had found something only to have it not pan out in the end.

Buzz spent the evening going around and talking to his people. He told them that the forensic team would be able to tell them something more positive in the morning. He also told them to be patient and to get some rest so they could get back on it in the morning.

The door to Wolff and Mugabe's cell crashed open and Frank Sylvan appeared in the doorway, a big-bore semiautomatic pistol in his hand. "You," he said pointing the weapon at Wolff. "Back up against the wall."

Wolff got up from the floor and did as he was told. "What's going on?"

Sylvan followed his movements with the pistol. "Shut up!" he snapped.

A man with a medical bag entered the cell and Wolff relaxed. Apparently the pilot's appeal had finally worked. But he also realized that it had worked because whoever was in charge of this operation only wanted them to stay alive so they could be killed later.

Without speaking, the medic quickly helped Mojo out of the top of his flight suit and examined his arm. "It's not bad," he told Sylvan, "He's just dislocated it."

"Do what you have to and be quick about it," Sylvan snapped.

Mojo bit his lip as the medic roughly manipulated the dislocation back into place. Usually this was done with pain medication, but apparently the concern of their captors didn't extend as far as to provide that kind of comfort for the wounded man.

"Jesus!" Mugabe said softly when he tried to move his arm as soon as the medic was finished.

"Don't move it," the medic said. "I've got to put it in a sling first."

Since he had been successful with getting the medic, Wolff tried for another concession while the man was putting Mojo's arm in the sling. "Can we get us a couple of beds in here?" he asked Sylvan. "We're going to catch cold sleeping on the floor."

Sylvan looked at him for a long moment. "You'd better watch your fucking mouth, cop," he snarled, his lips compressed tightly. Sylvan could barely stand to look at a cop, much less talk to one.

Wolff shrugged and looked innocent. "I'm just trying to keep us in good health."

Sylvan looked down at the medic who was just tying off the sling. "You about done?"

"Yeah."

"Move it then."

The medic withdrew and Sylvan closed the door behind them and locked it.

"How does it feel?" Wolff asked.

Mojo wiggled his fingers. "It feels a whole lot better than it did," he answered. "I don't know where that guy went to school, but he knows what he's doing."

Wolff sat down on the floor beside him. "Do you get the feeling that whoever these guys are, they really don't like cops?"

"The thought had crossed my mind."

A few minutes later the door opened again and one of the guards handed in two army surplus canvas cots and a couple of blankets.

"Thanks," Wolff said.

The guard didn't answer as he slammed the metal door shut. Wolff heard the rattle of the padlock as he snapped it back in place.

"This is getting to look more and more like the Hilton every day," Wolff said as he quickly set up the bunks on each side of the room. "I may decide to extend my reservation here a while longer."

"It's more like the Hanoi Hilton, you mean," Mugabe corrected him, referring to the notorious North Vietnamese prison camps of thirty or so years ago.

"At least we'll be sleeping up off the floor for a change," Wolff said, glancing over at the big plastic bucket they had been given to use as a latrine. "Now all we have to do is to improve the sanitary facilities."

"At least we don't have to dump it," Mojo pointed out with a smirk.

109

Wolff laughed. "That's a good job for these guys all right, latrine detail."

"You know," Mojo said as he stretched out on his bunk. "This kind of makes me feel like when I was back in basic training. I had a drill instructor who would take our bunks away when we were bad boys and make us sleep on the floor. "Extra training," he called it. Those bunks sure felt good when we got back in them after spending a week on the cold, hard concrete floor."

"They didn't do shit like that to us at Blue U," Wolff said, remembering his short tenure at the Air Force Academy. "We were all supposed to be future officers and gentlemen, so when our drill sergeants were pissed off at use they made us march around in square circles all night with our rifles and full packs."

"I sure could do with a rifle and a pack right about now," Mojo flexed his bad arm.

"I'd settle for just the rifle," Wolff laughed. "Not to mention a basic load of ammunition. They can keep the fucking pack."

"And a hacksaw," Mojo added.

"I think we're going to need more than that to get out of this place," Wolff said, looking at the steel door. "Maybe a cutting torch."

"No matter what we need to get out," Mojo shook his head, "it sure as hell doesn't look like we're going to find it in here."

Wolff lay back on his cot and put his hands behind his head. "You've got that right, partner."

Chapter Fourteen

The Forest Service Airstrip; 26 December

It was late afternoon the day after Christmas before Buzz was able to get a forensic team up from the Denver TPF field office. The minute that their small jet touched down on the landing strip, the three police technicians were quickly bundled into cold weather gear and hustled on board Gunner's Dragon One Four for the short flight up to the deserted cabin.

Once on site, a four-man team from Zoomie's Tac Platoon secured the area while the forensic team methodically took the small cabin apart looking for anything that might tell them if the two missing men had been there. When they had completed their search, they boarded the chopper to fly back to the airstrip to put their samples through the small lab they had brought with them.

To prevent his own people from interfering with the technicians before they were finished with their delicate work, Buzz posted one of Zoomie's men in front of the small tent they were using as a lab to keep everyone away. He also had to resist the urge to stand behind them himself and look over their shoulders.

Everyone was anxious to hear what the lab results had to say. Even though the waiting was hard, they were all just going to have to wait. But while they were waiting, the Griffins were high over the forest again continuing the visual search. Wolff and Mugabe were still out there somewhere, and the Tac Force couldn't rest until they were found.

"I wonder why they're feeding us this shit?" Wolff asked as he tore open the survival ration pack the guards had thrown into their cell for lunch. "They've got to have a mess hall somewhere in here that's serving real food. They can't be on a tight budget, not with an operation like this."

"They're feeding us the food we brought with us," Mugabe said, stating the obvious.

"But why?" Wolff frowned. "I know they can't be eating this kind of shit themselves."

"They're feeding us this shit," Mojo explained, "so that when they finally do an autopsy the coroner won't find something in our stomachs that didn't come from our survival rations."

"How'd you figure that one out?" Wolff asked, letting the opened ration fall on his bunk.

"You know that my dad was a doctor," Mojo answered, taking a bite out of his lunch. "Well, along with his regular practice, he also did forensic work on the side for extra money."

"That's one hell of a way to make a few extra coins," Wolff frowned, staring down at his meal. "Cutting up dead people."

"True," Mojo pointed out. "But if he hadn't done that, I wouldn't know that these guys are real serious about killing us sometime in the very near future."

"The thing I can't figure out," Wolff said, still not eating his meal, "is why? What are they doing here? What is so goddamned important here that it's worth the risk of killing two Federal cops?"

"Beats the shit outta me," Mugabe said. "But this is no nickel-and-dime operation we're dealing with here, my man. It takes a shitload of money to build something like this in the middle of a national forest right under the noses of the Forest Service."

"But what's it for?" Wolff repeated. "What's the purpose of all this? Why in the hell would anyone build a hideout like this under a mountain? That's what I can't figure out. What in the hell are they doing in here?"

"I haven't the slightest," Mojo said, licking up the last of the crumbs. "But whatever it is, they sure as hell don't want us saying anything about it."

"Which means," Wolff said, "that we'd better start getting our shit together and figure out how in the hell we're going to get our asses out of here."

Mojo raised one eyebrow. "And just how do you plan to do that?"

Wolff shrugged and shook his head. "Beats me, man, but we've got to do something real soon before they decide to put us into permanent cold storage."

"While you're thinking about what we're going to do," Mojo said, "I'll eat your lunch if you're not hungry. No point in letting it go to waste."

Wolff handed the packet over without a word. Lunch was the least of his worries right now. Thinking about freezing to death had ruined his appetite.

"You know, this stuff actually isn't all that bad," Mojo said halfway through Wolff's lunch. "You kinda develop a taste for it."

"How in the hell can you just sit there and eat that stuff?!" Wolff exploded.

Mojo crammed the last of the survival bar in his mouth and shrugged his shoulders. "What else am I going to do in here? Run laps?"

Buzz held a pilots' meeting later that evening in the mess hall tent. The tent was crowded to overflowing. Everyone from the air crew to the cooks wanted to hear what the lab boys had learned.

"Okay, listen up," Buzz said as he stepped into the middle of the tent, a thick report in his hand. "I've got good news and bad news."

The assembled chopper cops quickly quieted down and took their seats.

"The forensic team has finished their preliminary report on what was found at the cabin. For one, they did not pick up any clear fingerprints at the site, but there's a couple of partials and they're being enhanced and run through the computer right now."

"Second, all they have for boot prints is again only a partial found in the dust under the stove. They think the print came from someone who was standing close to the stove to get warm. The shape does match the curvature of the toe of a size eleven TPF flight boot, which is the same size boot that Wolff wears."

Cheering broke out and Buzz let his people go on for a moment or two.

"Okay," he said, finally holding his hand up. "That's enough."

When the crowd finally settled down, he continued with his briefing. "That toe profile, however, also matches several other kinds of hiking boots, so that's not much to go on. There wasn't enough of the print left to pick up any of the sole pattern."

He thumbed through the report. "Next, fiber sampling didn't reveal much either. Most of what they found seems to have been there for quite some time. They did, however, find a small fragment of plastic sheeting, silver on one side and dull black on the other."

He paused for a moment. "The same colors as the space blankets found in our survival kits."

The room broke out in cheers again.

"But," he held up his hand and continued, "the manufacturer who supplies us with that item also sells identical space blankets on the civilian market. And right now we don't have a positive ID on it as being from the Griffin's survival kit."

"Actually, our best piece of information is negative information. According to the lab guys, the cabin had been swept clean recently. Exactly when they can't tell, but there was no spring pollen found in the dust and very little dust or dirt on the floor at all."

Buzz looked up from the report. "Wolff and Mugabe were not known for their housekeeping skills, so we don't think that they cleaned up after themselves."

That brought another round of laughs, which helped to break the tension.

"And last we come to the firewood situation," Buzz continued. "According to the report, the ashes in the stove were fairly recent, not older than a couple of weeks. They can't get it any closer than that with the gear they brought with them. The same goes for the broken edges on the furniture."

"But," he held up his hand, "this does not necessarily mean that Wolff and Mugabe burned the wood. It may be that some skier came by, built the fire, and swept the place out before spending the night and moving on. We just don't know at this time. There may be more of that later. The forensic team will take the samples back to Denver and continue working on them there."

Buzz thumbed through the report to see if there was anything he had missed. "That's about it," he said. "We've got everyone in the western region, including the supermarket tabloid psychics, working on this one, and I'll let you know anything they find out ASAP."

"What do the psychics say?" someone in the back of the tent shouted.

Buzz grinned broadly. "The latest survey taken has it that Mojo and the Wolfman were kidnapped by aliens from Mars and taken to a mother ship orbiting on the dark side of the moon. The minority opinion, however, is that they have slipped through a time warp and were sent back to the Old West to rescue Elvis."

That got a laugh out of most of the people, but Gunner was not amused. "Fucking assholes," he growled.

"Buzz is just trying to lighten things up a little," Legs said. "To ease the tension."

"This isn't fucking funny," he replied. "Not one damned bit. Those guys could be dying right now and he's making fucking jokes."

"He knows that," Legs explained. "He's just as worried as the rest of us, but he's trying to keep it under control. Give him a break, Gunner."

"I still don't think it's funny."

"Are there any questions?" Buzz asked, looking around the tent. "If not, the mission for tomorrow is the same as it was today: keep on looking and report anything you see."

Looking out over the crowded tent, he spotted Sandra and Gunner sitting off to one side. "Officers Revell and Jennings, I want to see you after this. The rest of you, go back to work."

"What's up, sir?" Gunner asked when he and Sandra walked up to their commander.

Buzz thumbed through the report in his hand. "Remember the guy that you two let beat up on you in Grimsley—Sunderland, Leroy P.? Well, it seems that he got himself iced in the Denver Detention Center last night."

"What!" Sandra had a shocked expression on her face. "What did he do?"

Buzz shrugged. "They don't know, but it looks like he really pissed someone off. Someone stuffed a sock in his mouth, beat him severely, and then cut most of his face off before slitting his throat."

"That sounds like a Family hit," Gunner frowned. "What is the Mob doing messing around with a jerk like that from some hick town in Colorado?"

"That's what we're looking into right now," Buzz said. "We're very interested in the answer to that particular question."

"How about the other guy?" Sandra asked. "The bartender with the sawed-off shotgun?"

"He's been moved into protective custody," Buzz answered. "And he's being questioned, but he claims that he doesn't know anything about it. He also claims that he didn't even know the victim."

"If that's the case," Sandra frowned, "then I don't understand why in the hell he would do something as stupid as pull a piece on me. That doesn't make any sense unless he was trying to protect the other guy."

"That's how I see it," Buzz said. "And that's why the interrogation team is asking him that very same question right now."

"I know it's a long shot," Sandra said hesitantly, "but do you think there could possibly be some kind of connection between that Sunderland guy and our not being able to find Wolff and Mojo?"

Buzz's face softened. He reached out and touched her arm in a fatherly way. "Sandra, we're all worried about Wolff and Mugabe, but we have no reason to think that they are anything other than simply lost in the woods somewhere. I don't think there's any connection between their crash and what happened to you and Jennings."

117

"I know," she said. "But we haven't been able to find a single trace of them except for that cabin. This whole thing's just too weird. It's like they dropped off the face of the earth. Maybe someone found them first and is holding them captive."

Now Buzz frowned. "We don't have any evidence of that," he said. "And we need to be very careful about what we say. We can't afford to have rumors about things like that getting started. The press would have a field day with something like that."

She looked up at Buzz with a tight smile. "I haven't said anything about this to anyone else. And don't worry, I'll keep my ideas to myself."

Chapter Fifteen

The Forest Service Airstrip; 27 December

The Griffins that took off for the early morning flight left without Gunner and Legs. Red's people had found a leaking hydraulic pump when they had serviced their chopper the night before and they were waiting for a replacement part to be flown up from Denver.

"Jesus, Red," Gunner said. "I thought you people kept stuff like that on hand."

Red took the dead cigar out of his mouth and spit a thin stream of tobacco juice on the floor of the maintenance tent. "Do you have any idea of just how many fucking pieces there on that goddamned bird?" He continued without giving Gunner a chance to answer the question. "Or how many replacement parts we have to stock for a forward operation like this?"

He stuck the cigar back into his mouth, "Well, I'll tell you. I have over five thousand line items, and every goddamned one of them . . ."

Gunner took another drink of his coffee and tuned Red's tirade out. He didn't have time for his excuses, all he wanted to hear from him was when One Four would be airworthy again so he could get back at it. As far as he was concerned, if the maintenance chief had been doing his job, this wouldn't have happened. Someone would have spotted this problem before it became a problem.

119

". . . and considering how many hours you and Legs have been putting on that machine the last couple of days, I'm not surprised that she's coming apart at the seams. That damned thing wasn't designed to fly twenty-four hours a day. It's got to be worked on sometimes."

Red took the cigar out of his mouth again. "And speaking of working up here, do you have any idea what kind of strain this weather's putting on my people? Well, let me tell you . . ."

"I don't want to hear it, Red," Gunner snapped, slamming his cup down on the makeshift desk. "Just get off your dead ass and get One Four back up in the air so I can go back to work."

Red's eyes narrowed and his teeth clamped down on his cigar butt. "You little . . ."

The piercing warble of the alert siren cut through Red's angry retort. Both men jumped up and headed for the door of the tent at a dead run.

Gunner pushed Red out of the way and dashed across the frozen ground for his ship. A mechanic was still working on something and the engine cowling was open. "Can this thing fly?" Gunner yelled up to him.

The skinny mechanic pulled his head out from under the cowling and blinked. "Ah . . . it's got that hydraulic leak, Gunner."

"I don't care about the fucking leak," Gunner shouted back. "Can it fly?"

"Sure," the mechanic answered. "I can just top off the hydraulic fluid reservoir and . . ."

"Do it fast!" Gunner yelled as he slid open the pilot's door and scrambled into his seat. Jamming his flight helmet on his head, he flipped on the internal power and keyed his throat mike. "Dragon Control, this is One Four on the flight line. What's the alert?"

"One Four," came Mom's voice over his head phones.

"Send status."

Gunner saw Legs racing across the airstrip, zipping up her flight jacket as she ran. "This is One Four, I'm go in two minutes."

"Control, copy," she answered. "We have a Code Twenty. One Three is taking fire at two, three, six-seven, three, four. How copy?"

Legs was scrambling into her seat and buckling her shoulder harness as Gunner keyed the numbers into their navigation computer. "One Four, copy Code Twenty. What's his situation?"

"We don't know at this time," Mom replied. "But he reports that he's taking gunfire from that area. As soon as you arrive at that location, take control of Dragon Flight and get it sorted out."

"One Four, copy. Cranking now."

Gunner leaned out of the open door and yelled up to the mechanic. "Button this fucker up, we've got to go!"

The mechanic slid down onto the stub wing, lowered the cowling, and latched it in place. "Go!" he shouted, slamming the palm of his hand against the armored skin.

"Clear!" Gunner yelled to warn the mechanics as he slammed his door shut and hit the start trigger on the collective stick.

The portside starter motor whined and the turbine ignited with a whoosh of burning kerosene. As the compressor blades spooled up to flight idle speed, Gunner switched over and fired up the other turbine. Overhead, the four-bladed rotor slowly started turning.

"Come on! Come on!" Gunner muttered impatiently, his eyes fixed on his turbine and rotor RPM gauges as the needles climbed up into the green.

In the left-hand seat, Sandra had activated her tactical screen and was downloading the target information from Dragon One Three. As soon as the light started blinking to indicate that the data had been transmitted, she activated her monitor and looked at the video scene being transmitted from One Three.

The other chopper was orbiting high above some kind of compound built well back under the trees. Several cinder block buildings formed a hollow square, and as she watched, she saw small figures darting out from under the trees, aiming what looked like assault rifles up at the chopper and firing before dashing back into cover. The shots weren't reaching the high-flying Griffin, but it looked like something out of a war movie.

Whatever it was, One Three had stirred up some kind of a hornet's nest.

As soon as the rotor came up to speed, Gunner keyed his mike as he twisted the throttle up against the stop and pushed forward on his cyclic control stick. "Dragon Control, this is One Four. We're taking off now."

"Control, copy."

The Griffin lunged forward, her tail high as her turbines screamed and her rotor blades fought for lift in the thin, cold mountain air. A hundred meters down the runway, Gunner hauled up on the collective control stick, turning the edges of the blades deeper into the air and sending the gunship rocketing up into the sky.

"ETA Code Twenty location twenty-six minutes," he radioed. "Have One Two meet me there."

"Control, copy," Mom replied. "He'll be there as soon as the Tac Platoon gets loaded on. Good hunting."

With her turbines screaming at overrev, Gunner sent his ship racing over the snow-covered forest. For the first time since they had arrived up here, he had something to do that he knew would be successfully taken care of. Nobody shot at TPF choppers and got away with it.

* * *

As Gunner and Sandra approached the Code Twenty site Sandra spotted Browning and Simpson in One Three orbiting high in the sky, well above the range of effective small arms fire. "One Three," Gunner radioed to him, "this is One Four. What do you have down there?"

"This is One Three," Browning radioed back. "I'm not quite sure. It looks like a fortified compound with maybe three houses and some outbuildings. I was flying over it to check it out when these guys suddenly started firing at me."

"Did you get hit?"

"This is One Three. We took a few rounds on the armor, but everything's still in the green."

"One Four," Gunner radioed back. "Copy. Those buildings look like they may be housing families in there, so stay out of range until I get back to Command One. I don't want anyone to get hurt who doesn't deserve it."

"One Three, copy."

Gunner got on the radio back to the airstrip and quickly updated Buzz on the situation.

"Copy," Buzz called back. "Wait till Zoomie's people get here in One Two, and then I want you to fly over and give them a chance to surrender. Under no circumstances are you to fire unless you have a clear target that is threatening you or another officer. ROE Alpha is now in effect until further notice. How copy?"

Gunner grimaced when he heard Buzz impose Rules of Engagement Alpha. That was going to make their job a hell of a lot tougher. The Tac Force had three levels of deadly force, governed by the Alpha, Bravo, and Charlie rules of engagement. ROE Alpha only allowed the use of weapons to save a life; Bravo allowed the Tac cops to shoot back at anyone who shot at them; and Charlie was a shoot-on-sight order and was rarely ever authorized except in extreme circumstances.

Under ROE Alpha, they were going to have to go into an armed camp and try to put the situation in order without using deadly force. This was not going to be fun. "One Four, good copy," Gunner acknowledged.

The two Griffins flew a high orbit around the compound for fifteen minutes until One Two showed up with half of the Tac Platoon in the back.

"One Two," Gunner radioed, "this is One Four. Maintain orbit here while Browning and I go in and try to talk to these guys."

"One Two, copy."

While One Two flew well off to the side, Gunner and One Three banked off to make a low-level pass down over the compound. One Three led the way while Gunner and Sandra flew five hundred meters behind them and off to one side to give them fire support if they needed it.

In the left-hand seat of One Four, Sandra's fingers were wrapped around the firing controls to her chain gun, and her helmet face shield's optical sight was cranked all the way up to maximum magnification. She had switched the 25mm chain gun in the nose turret over to single-shot operation, and with the high magnification sight was now ready to use the weapon as an aerial sniper's rifle.

All she had to do was to fix the target in the sight reticle and the autostabilized gun would do all the rest. The weapon automatically reaimed itself at the target ten times a second, and on single-shot fire was deadly. Even though the 25mm chain gun was a bit large for a sniping weapon, it was more accurate than most rifles. She wasn't as good at single-shot fire as Mojo was, but she felt that she could adequately protect One Three when they made their low-level loudspeaker run.

"Okay," Gunner radioed as they approached the compound, "Read 'em the Riot Act."

Browning switched on the external loudspeakers on the belly of his ship and keyed his throat mike. "This is the Tactical Police Force," his voice boomed over the snow-covered forest. "Lay down your weapons and . . ."

Two men stepped out from under the trees and raised their rifles to their shoulders to aim at One Three. Sandra sighted in on the one on the left and squeezed the trigger. Before bothering to see if she had hit her first target, she switched over to the other man, centered the sight reticle on his chest, and pulled the trigger again. Both men went down, one after the other, their upper bodies smashed. Even a nonexplosive 25mm round can ruin your whole day.

No sooner had Sandra fired than Gunner was on the radio. "One Three, get the hell outta there!"

The chopper abruptly broke away to the right as the pilot twisted his throttle up all the way. Puffs of smoke from the trees indicated that more people were shooting at him, but Sandra couldn't find any specific targets and was forced to hold her fire while Gunner broke left and raced back out of range.

Safely back in their high orbit, Gunner reported back to Buzz, who gave the word to move the Tac Platoon in to get this sorted out. He didn't know why these people had fired on the Griffins, but it had to be stopped.

In the back of One Two, Zoomie had been following the action on the remote monitor in the rear compartment. It showed everything that the targeting computers on the other two Griffins picked up on video. He monitored Buzz's orders and knew that subduing that place was going to be a bitch. He didn't have enough men with him to do the job, and he was going to have to call in the rest of the Tac Platoon.

"Dragon Lead," Zoomie called over to Gunner. "This is

Tac One, come in."

"One Four, go ahead."

"This is Tac One. Tell Command One that I need the rest of my people up here ASAP. I've got a lot of ground to cover and don't have enough men to do it with. How about having One Three drop off his search team and then go back to pick up the rest of the Tac Platoon?"

"This is One Four, copy." Gunner replied. "Coordinate directly with them on this."

"Tac One," Browning's voice broke in. "This is One Three. I monitored. Where do you want me to drop off the search team?"

Zoomie keyed in a location on the screen and transmitted the data to One Three.

"Good copy," Browning called back as soon as the location showed up on his navigation screen. "We'll be there in zero two."

With that taken care of, Zoomie ordered his pilot to put them down at that location as well. It was time to get this show on the road.

Zoomie dropped off one of his men to augment the search team and then had his pilot fly them on to yet another location a third of the distance along a big circle around the center of the compound, where he dropped off half of his remaining men. At the third and last location, Zoomie himself got out with his remaining three men.

Now he had three teams on the ground surrounding the compound in a rough circle. When the rest of the Tac Platoon arrived they would be inserted to close off the spaces between the three teams, but for now he had enough people on the ground to go to work. The plan was that they would go in on three axes to clear the woods before meeting in the center to have a little chat with these guys about shooting at TPF helicopters.

Zoomie had given absolutely no thought as to why these people should be shooting at Dragon Flight's Griffins; all he knew was that they had fired first. Whatever their problem was, though, he was confident that his people would be the ones to fire the last shots.

"Okay, boys," he keyed his helmet mike. "Move it out and everybody watch yourselves. Remember we're in ROE Alpha and these assholes have got to be crazy."

Chapter Sixteen

Deep in the Forest; 27 December

Zoomie's three teams kept in close radio contact as they made their way through the snow-covered forest toward the compound. Overhead, the two Griffins flew high top cover, using their targeting sensors to spot potential targets for the Tac Platoon. This was not the time for any unpleasant surprises.

So far the woods were clean, but Zoomie was not encouraged by this lack of contact. He was all too aware they were moving into a hornet's nest, and he liked to have his enemies in plain sight. Also, he knew that his men were not really prepared for this kind of work today. Since they had been in a search and rescue mode, they were wearing their all-black uniforms. They showed up against the backdrop of snow like lumps of coal on a clean white sheet.

"One Four, Tac One," he radioed up to Gunner.

"One Four, go ahead."

"You got anything yet?"

"We've got movement right around the compound itself," Gunner reported. "But nothing coming your way."

"Copy," Zoomie answered. "When's One Three going to get here with the rest of my people?"

"His ETA's one zero."

"When they get here, have them break up into three teams," Zoomie ordered. "Four through Six, and drop them down in between the first three teams."

"Copy, I'll pass it on."

As soon as the other teams were in place, they could move a little faster and have a little better coverage of the area. Zoomie was anxious to get this shit over with as soon as they could. Maybe there was something to the rumor that had gotten started about Wolff and Mojo having been captured. There had to be some reason that these jerks had fired on One Three. Maybe these guys had captured them and were holding them prisoner.

"Tac One, this is One Four X-Ray," Sandra's voice came in over his helmet headphones.

"Tac One, go."

"You've got two men coming up on your front on a bearing of one two eight," she reported. "I read that they're packing iron and moving slowly from tree to tree."

"Copy," Zoomie called back, feeling his pulse start to beat faster. Here it was, his excitement for the trip, his adrenaline fix. "Can you cover me? I may need you to tag these guys if they get around me. My flanks are wide open."

"Copy," Sandra called back. "We'll be here."

Zoomie switched over to his team frequency and alerted the other three men with him, sending two of them farther out to the sides and bringing the third man in closer to him. It was pretty obvious that they were walking into an ambush, and he wanted to have a little backup.

"Tac One, this is X-Ray," came Sandra's voice again. "They've gone to ground some hundred and fifty meters in front of you on the other side of a small clearing. When you come out into the open, you'll be right in their sights."

That sounded like a great way to get sucker punched to Zoomie. There had to be a better way to deal with shit like that. "One Four X-Ray," he radioed. "Does ROE Alpha allow you to pop a little CN gas in the woods?"

Zoomie could hear Sandra's laughter over the radio. "That's most affirm, Tac One. I'm dialing in the gas grenades right now."

"Copy," Zoomie called back. "Give us time to put on our masks and get to the edge of the clearing, then drop it in their laps."

"One Four X-Ray, can do."

After donning their gas masks, Zoomie took the point position himself for the move to the edge of the clearing. Peering around the bottom of a large tree trunk, he couldn't see a thing but trees and drifted snow on the other side of the clearing. He dropped back down into cover and keyed his mike. "X-Ray, this is Tac One, are you sure those guys're over there? I can't spot 'em."

"They're down there all right," Sandra replied. "I've got them on visual. They're both wearing snowsuits and they're carrying scoped rifles that look like heavy-caliber military hardware."

The news about the sniper scopes made Zoomie hug his tree trunk a little tighter. He hated it when the bad guys were better equipped than he was. "Okay," he said. "Any time you're ready, do it to 'em."

"One Four X-Ray, on the way."

The faint sound of rotors grew louder in the cold air. Zoomie looked up through the trees and saw One Four diving on the other side of the clearing. The nose turret winked fire as the 40mm grenade launcher spit CN gas grenades at the slow rate of fire, fifty rounds a minute.

The edge of the clearing blossomed with small puffs of black smoke, followed by billowing clouds of thick white CN gas. Through the clouds of gas, Zoomie saw two figures stagger to their feet and try to run. Running only sucked more gas into their lungs, and both men dropped to their hands and knees in the snow.

130

They were still coughing, hacking and fighting to breathe, when Zoomie and his backup raced up to them. "Freeze!" Zoomie shouted. "One move and you're dead!"

With his backup covering them, Zoomie quickly bound each man's hands behind him with plastic restraints and then dragged them up to their feet.

Keying his throat mike, Zoomie called up for Gunner to land and take charge of his prisoners. Two down and he hadn't even had to fire a shot.

As soon as the two prisoners had been secured in the rear compartment restraints in One Four, Gunner took off to take up his top cover position again and Zoomie checked in with his other teams.

By this time, One Three had returned and had put the rest of the Tac teams in place. Now that Zoomie had all of his platoon on the ground, he tightened the ring around the forest compound. He didn't want any of these guys to slip past them and get away in the woods. Whoever these assholes were, he wanted to have a nice long talk with each and every one of them.

The Tac Platoon's movement through the woods was not interrupted by any more surprises until they got within sight of the compound. The going had been slow, however, and night was falling as they formed up into a big circle some three hundred meters across. Even though it was dark, the men were spread out so evenly that no one could possibly get past them without being spotted by the night vision equipment.

From a covered position behind a tree trunk, Zoomie used his night vision glasses to check out the compound he had first seen from the chopper. Up close it looked even worse than it did from the air. It was a maze of concrete block and rough log houses, sheds, and what looked like a big barn. A small, well-armed group hiding behind those thick walls could hold off a much larger force than he had with him.

Now that Zoomie knew exactly what they were up against, he wanted to see if he could settle this thing the easy way. He knew that if he sent his people into the maze of buildings to dig those guys out someone was going to get hurt, and it wouldn't be only the bad guys. Also, he could see a children's playset under one of the trees. Further evidence that there were families living in there.

He keyed his mike and reported his findings back to Buzz at the CP. Buzz radioed back with permission for Zoomie to try to talk the people out of their houses. "Remember, though," he cautioned, "if you can't, don't let it get out of hand. You're under ROE Alpha for this operation."

"Tac One, copy."

The Griffins had been holding back well out of the line of sight while the Tac Platoon made their approach. Now that it was dark and the troops were in place, they could move in closer to support the operation. With their navigation lights off and their mirror skin turned to dull black, they were impossible to spot against the moonless sky.

Zoomie called up to One Four and had Sandra plug his radio signal into the chopper's audio system. Once he was linked to the loudspeakers, he called out.

"In the compound," Zoomie's amplified voice boomed through the trees. "This is the Tactical Police Force. We have you completely surrounded. We will not fire on you if you surrender peacefully. Come out with your hands up over your heads and we will hold our fire."

The muzzle of an assault rifle appeared in one of the windows and opened up on the Griffin with a burst of full automatic fire. The bullets sparked as they bounced off the Griffin's belly armor.

A roar of return fire from the Tac Platoon positions answered the assault rifle, shattering the window and splintering the frame around it. The fire from the house ceased abruptly.

"Check fire! Check fire!" Zoomie yelled into his radio. "There's women and kids in there!"

The Tac cops ceased fire instantly.

After checking in with the chopper to see if it had suffered any damage, Zoomie put in a conference call to all of his team leaders to inform them of the revised situation.

"What do we do, sir?" Sergeant Garcia asked.

"Smoke 'em out," the second team leader suggested. "A few CN grenades in each building should take care of it quite nicely."

"We can't use gas," Zoomie said. "Adults can usually survive a good dose of CN, but it might hurt the kids."

"How about using flash bang grenades?" Garcia suggested. "Those shouldn't hurt the kids. They'll scare the hell outta them, yes, but they won't kill them."

Zoomie thought for a moment. "Okay, let's give them a try. But we've still got to be careful; I don't want to hit any civilians by mistake."

Zoomie called up to the Griffins and had one of them go into a hover, lined up on the first building in front of them. On his command, the gunship started firing its grenade launcher, carefully placing a flash bang grenade into each window.

The Tac cops got to their feet and rushed the building. Crouching under the broken windows, they pitched more flash bang grenades through the broken glass. As soon as the grenades detonated, with a blinding flash and ear-splitting explosion, the teams went through the windows after them, their night vision goggles turned up all the way and their H&Ks at the ready.

The ground floor was empty, but as they started for the stairs they heard noises from the upper floor. The team

133

leader called for his grenadier and had the man fire another flash bang grenade up the stairwell. A man screamed and staggered out to the top of the stairs. "Don't shoot!" he shouted. "I give up!"

After taking the man into custody, the team swept through the rest of the top floor. It was empty except for the body of the man who had shot at the Griffin.

Zoomie had just taken the message that the house had been cleared with no losses, one body, and one prisoner when the next building in front of him suddenly burst into flames. In the flickering light of the flames, Zoomie saw a figure dart out the door, a rifle in his hands. The fire made the Tac Platoon's night vision devices useless, so Zoomie sighted in on him through his H&K's iron sights and held the sight picture. If the guy dropped his piece it would be okay. But if he didn't, sorry about that . . .

The man stopped a few steps away from the door, squinted into the darkness, and raised his rifle. Zoomie tightened his finger around the trigger and the rifle spat. The man gave a cry and went over onto his face.

The next building behind it suddenly burst into flames as well. Zoomie smelled burning gasoline and frowned. What in the hell was going on here? Were these people burning the buildings themselves?

He was clicking on his throat mike to ask the Griffins to turn on their searchlights so he could see what was going on when a hail of gunfire broke out from behind the second building. The Tac team on the far side of the circle quickly returned the fire. A sharp fight went on for a few minutes, and the team leader reported that a small group of armed men were trying to fight their way out of the circle.

The firing died off and Zoomie was taking the report when two men, their assault rifles firing from the hip, raced out from behind the building toward Zoomie's team. Outlined by the fires behind them, the two made perfect targets. A short flurry of fire cut them both down.

With that final burst, silence fell over the compound. All that was heard was the snapping and cracking of the flames and the faint *wop-woping* sounds of the Griffins overhead. Zoomie didn't know how many people were still out there and decided to try to talk to them one last time. He called up to the chopper and linked into the audio system again.

"Come out with your hands up," Zoomie's voice boomed over the compound again. "We will not shoot if you come out with your hands up."

A figure stumbled out into the open and Zoomie sighted in on him. Through the rifle sights, he saw that the man had his hands in the air over his head.

"Don't shoot!" the man yelled. "We give up!"

"Come on over here," Zoomie yelled. "Hurry!"

He called up to the choppers and had them turn on their searchlights. The beams spotlighted a small group, the man and two women with several children hanging onto their skirts or clutched in their arms.

"Over here!" Zoomie stood up and motioned them forward. When the people got to his position, he pulled them all down into cover.

"How many more of you are in there?" the platoon leader asked urgently.

The man shook his head. "I don't rightly know," he said. "There was a couple of wounded guys in the main house and I ain't seen Jim and Sam since noon."

"How many woman and children?" Zoomie asked again.

One of the women spoke up. "The rest of the women are in the big bunker with their kids," she said. "Joshua told us to hide in there because you'd kill us all if we didn't."

"Where is this bunker?"

"Under the back of the big barn."

Zoomie got on his radio and dispatched two of the Tac teams to the barn. One team was to search for the people

135

while the other provided security for them. Just because this one group had surrendered did not necessarily mean that the rest of them were ready to give up yet.

The search team quickly radioed back that they had found a dozen or so women and children in the bunker and were taking them into custody. Now that the women and children were safe, Zoomie sent the rest of his people on a sweep of the compound for anyone else who wanted to argue with the Tac Force.

Chapter Seventeen

The Survivalist's Compound; 28 December

Next morning, the chill air carried thin wisps of smoke rising from the wreckage of the compound as the Tac Platoon searched through the rubble for any sign that Wolff and Mugabe had been held captive by the survivalists. As Zoomie searched with them, he could not comprehend why these people would have wanted to burn their own buildings down.

He shook his head. There was no accounting for the way some people thought. He couldn't even figure why they had wanted to live so far out in the middle of nowhere in the first place.

The survivors of last night's firefight were currently being interrogated. But all that had been learned was that the compound had been some kind of religious survivalist community. Families who had gotten as far away from civilization as they could in order to survive the Apocalypse, which would herald the coming of the new millennium. They still had not found out why these people had fired on the choppers in the first place, and they had not learned anything from them about the missing men.

The TPF interrogators were pressing them hard for information about Wolff and Mugabe, but none of them claimed to know anything about them. When the men were asked why they had fired on the Griffins, they answered that Joshua, their leader, had told them that God wanted them to do it. He had said that the choppers were the agents of Satan who were coming to take them from their wilderness paradise.

When one of the men was asked why he didn't find out who was in the choppers before he shot at it, he looked surprised, as if that thought had never occurred to him.

Zoomie walked over to the interrogation area as the man who had been the first to surrender was being questioned.

"Why did you shoot at us?" the interrogator asked.

The man shrugged. "Joshua told us to," he said. "He told us that you were the agents of Satan."

"What the hell's wrong with you people?" Zoomie broke in. He was still angry that the women and children had been endangered. "You could see our TPF markings on the bottoms of the choppers."

"We always do what Joshua tells us to."

"Were you holding anyone prisoner in there?" the interrogator asked, changing the subject. "Maybe a couple of police officers?"

The man looked puzzled. "No," he answered slowly. "Not that I know about."

"What do you mean," Zoomie asked, "not that you know about?"

The man looked up at him. "Joshua did lots of things that he never told us about until afterward," he said. "Sometimes God told him to do something and he would do it. Later he would tell us what he had done."

"Like what?"

"Like when he made those two hikers disappear."

The two cops looked at each other. "What hikers?" Zoomie asked.

"A couple of kids, college kids, I guess, came by last year before the snow fell. They said they had lost most of their food to the bears and asked if they could buy some food from us. Joshua refused to sell them any and told them to

138

leave. Later one of us saw their backpacks hidden in the barn and we asked him about them. Joshua got that look in his eyes and said that God had told him to silence them or they would tell the agents of Satan where we were." The man shrugged. "I guess he killed them. I don't know."

Zoomie's face was grim. "Read this asshole his rights and book him along with all the rest of the adults. It looks like we may have us a homicide here as well as Federal firearms violations. I've got to call this in to Buzz."

It took most of the day to get the situation sorted out at the compound. All the suspects had to be airlifted to the CP site, and from there the Colorado State Police took them into custody. The children had to be looked after and a crime team was flown into the compound to sift through the wreckage.

All told, it had been a very busy day and a half, but when everyone had been thoroughly interrogated, there was still no news about Wolff and Mugabe. It looked like it was the same kind of wild-goose chase that the search of the cabin had been, and Zoomie was not amused. Not only had these assholes cost him an entire day, one of Zoomie's men had been hit and one of the choppers had received minor damage. The Tac cop was not badly wounded and the Griffin would be back in service in the morning, but that was not the point.

While they had been tied up dealing with these idiots, they had not been out in the woods looking for Mojo and the Wolfman.

Buck Sloan smiled as he tied the black bowtie around his neck. The CNN reporter was recounting the forest firefight between the TPF and the survivalists on the evening news. For the first time since the Tac Force had moved up into the national forest, it looked like things might be going his way. Even though the survivalists had had absolutely nothing to do with the two missing cops, the Tac Force didn't know that, and they were interrogating the survivors to see what they knew about them.

This incident was a great smokescreen, and it was working better than if Sloan had planned it himself. For the next couple of days the Tac Force would be so focused on those poor bastards that they wouldn't be any further trouble for him. And all he needed was to keep the cops busy for a few more days. He had received the final SDI satellite control codes today and was now ready to put New Dawn into operation as soon as New Year's Day rolled around. Once that happened, the Tac Force wouldn't be a problem for him anymore.

Slipping into his tuxedo jacket, he checked the time. While he was waiting for New Dawn, he still had to keep up with the day-to-day activities of a presidential candidate—a winning candidate, he reminded himself. The polls showed a dramatic increase in his popularity since the Tac Force had rounded up the protestors in the woods. As much trouble as the chopper cops had caused him lately, they still had their uses. He could always use them as an example of what was wrong in the United States today.

He decided that he would make some reference to them in his speech tonight, maybe tie it in with the brutal repression of that survivalist community. That would be a good touch, he thought as he walked over to his desk and pushed the call button on his intercom. Mattiese would have to change the text of his speech right away. He was due on stage in less than an hour.

"Yes, Buck?" The campaign manager appeared in the door.

"Did you see that news item about the Tac Force tonight?"

"That confrontation with the survivalists?"

"Right," Buck said. "I need to say something about that tonight. You know, deploring the use of excessive force, that sort of thing."

"Are you sure that you want to do that, Buck?" Mattiese frowned. "Those people are under indictment for the murder of several people over this last year."

"I still think that they could have been arrested in a more peaceful manner," Buck replied. "Burning down those houses is inexcusable."

Mattiese tried once more to change his boss's mind. "Buck, it looks like they burned them down themselves."

Sloan fixed the smaller man with a glare. "I don't see it that way at all," he said.

The campaign manager sighed inwardly. "I'll get right on it, Buck."

Sloan watched Mattiese walk out. He was beginning to worry about his campaign manager and was glad that he knew nothing about the New Dawn project. Sloan would have to make sure that he never did learn anything, either. Maybe the Family could help him with that problem as well.

There were times when Sloan wished that there had been some other way for him to accomplish what he had wanted to do without having to get involved with the Family. They had been helpful in more ways than one—their vast wealth, their political influence, and their protection services. But the closer he got to implementing New Dawn, the more paranoid they had become.

They had wanted him to kill the two chopper cops he was holding in the satellite facility, but he had refused, insisting that he take care of it his way. They had finally agreed, but not before adding a typical warning that nothing had better go wrong. The Family was making it very difficult for him to do what had to be done, but he kept telling himself that it would be over soon.

The next two days passed slowly for the men and women of the Tac Force as they searched and re-searched the same

141

ground with no results. It had been a big letdown when nothing had turned up at the survivalists compound, and Dragon Flight was not taking it very well. Tempers flared and Red had been forced to take two of his crew out behind the maintenance tent for a short lesson in courtesy. Each time, he came back alone.

The flight crews and search teams were doing everything it was possible for humans to do, but it wasn't working. It was as if Wolff and Mojo had disappeared off the face of the earth.

Nor had the days passed quickly for Wolff and Mojo. Their confinement had been reduced to total monotony, broken only by two meals of survival rations a day and the guard changing the slop bucket every morning.

Mugabe's arm was still not working well. It didn't hurt as much, but he did not have a full range of motion. Wolff was concerned, but he knew there was no point in talking to their captors about it. They sure as hell weren't going to send Mugabe to a hospital to have it checked out.

Like prisoners will do, the two men spent most of the time talking. They talked about food, they talked about women, they talked about cars, and they talked about their lives. The one thing they did not talk about was Dragon Flight and the Tac Force. They still had no way of knowing if the room was bugged, and they did not want to give their captors any information that might compromise their unit's operations.

Both of them believed that Dragon Flight was still out there looking for them, but they didn't talk about that, either. They also knew that when they weren't found within a certain period of time, Buzz would have no choice but to go back to Denver without them. And when that finally happened, their captors would make good on their threat to kill them.

142

Regardless of what Buzz was doing, though, they both knew that it was going to be up to them to save themselves. But until a chance presented itself, they talked. The topic today was fuckups, personal and professional.

"And so there I was," Wolff continued the tale of his days in the Air Force Academy. "Humping the commandant's daughter on the top of her old man's big oak desk when the door opens and he walks in on us. I might have been able to talk my way out of it, but he had his wife with him as well as the district's congressman and his wife."

Wolff chuckled. "Have you ever tried to salute and pull your pants up at the some time?"

Mugabe smiled. He had heard several versions of this story over the years and they all ended the same way, with Wolff being thrown out of the academy. Sometimes he wondered just what had really happened.

No matter what it had been though, as far as Mugabe was concerned, up until now it had been worth it. Had Wolff gone on to be an air force officer, they never would have gotten together in the Tac Force and the world would have been a poorer place, as far as he was concerned.

"You ever regret that moment's passion?" Mugabe asked.

"Well, actually not," Wolff grinned. "Had her old man not walked in on us, I might have had to marry her. As it was, she married an upperclassman that fall and instantly gained a hundred and fifty pounds."

"Saved from a fate worse than death."

Wolff looked thoughtful for a moment. "Yeah," he said slowly. "I'm not sure that I'm cut out for sleeping with someone who weighs more than I do."

"Speaking of that," Mojo said. "Did I ever tell you about the time I got hooked up with . . ."

Chapter Eighteen

Buzz nursed yet another cup of bad coffee as he stood in the door of the CP tent and looked out over the Forest Service airstrip. The high mountain meadow did not look much like a winter wonderland now. A week's worth of men and equipment trampling over the place had churned it into a half-frozen, half-muddy quagmire. Outside, the support personnel were packing up and readying their equipment for the flight back home to Denver.

He had gotten the orders to go home the night before, straight from TPF Headquarters in Washington. He had spent a week looking for his two downed flyers, and beyond the shattered carcass of their Griffin and signs that they had stopped over at the cabin, nothing had been seen of either one of them. It was as if they had vanished off the face of the earth. By this time they had to be dead of starvation, if nothing else. No one dressed as they had been could have survived more than a few days in this cold.

Buzz would have liked to stay another week to continue searching for their bodies, but orders were orders. And deep in his heart, he knew that it was time that Dragon Flight got back to work.

The criminal element in their region wasn't taking a vacation while Dragon Flight was concentrating all of their efforts to look for the missing men. The war against the maggots went on, and they were back in the war. There had been a rash of armed bank robberies in the Phoenix — Tucson area that needed their attention, and there was information about another major drug lab in the woods of southern Oregon that should be looked into.

It was always tough to lose people, and it was doubly tough to lose them in this fashion. Had Wolff and Mojo finally gone down in a blaze of gunfire, Mojo's fingers on the triggers and the chain gun firing off the last of its ammunition, that would have been one thing. At least they would have taken someone with them. But to die like this, to disappear into the frozen, snow-covered forest without a trace and not even be able to be recover their bodies, that was a waste of two of the best cops who had ever worn golden police wings.

What a waste!

Buzz took another sip of his cold coffee and spit it out on the frozen ground. Christ! He knew better than to drink the shit Red brewed. What in the hell was wrong with him? He threw the last half cup of the coffee out into the snow and made a mental note to report that coffee spill to the Environmental Protection Agency. They'd have to get a pollution control team up here in the spring to take care of it. If they didn't, nothing would grow there for years.

He turned back to the tent and noticed that Mom was still sitting behind her commo console. When the old girl retired they'd have to perform surgery to remove her ass from that chair, and even then the scars would remain forever. Maybe it would be better to just bury her with her commo headset. When he approached her, he saw that her eyes were red from crying.

Jesus! Mom crying over Wolff and Mugabe? No way!

Buzz had also noticed that there was a distinct lack of hustle in everyone today. No one was ready to give up on Mojo and the Wolfman. He knew how they felt; he missed those two hot dogs too. Dragon Flight was not going to be the same without them. But damn it, there was work to be done. They had to accept their losses and get on with it.

He walked up behind Mom and hesitantly put his hands on the back of her chair. "We have to wrap it up now, Ruby," he said gently.

Mom spun around to face him, her headset still in place over her ears. "They're not dead, Buzz," she said softly. "I just know they're not dead."

"I don't believe it, either, Ruby," he replied. "I really don't, but they've been out there for over a week. If they'd just stayed put at the ship or even at the cabin, they'd be home now."

He got a puzzled look on his face. "I don't understand why in the hell they left that cabin. They had a stove, they were in out of the wind, it was a perfect place to ride out the storm till we could get to them. I just don't understand why they left."

"They were captured," Mom stated flatly. "That's the only thing that makes any sense to me. They left the ship because one of them was hurt and the other wanted to get help for him. And I think that it was Mojo who was hurt. Didn't you say that the Griffin's cabin ended up on the left side? The gunner's side?"

Buzz nodded.

"So, Wolff drags him out of the wreckage and carries him through the woods. How far was it from the crash to the cabin?"

"A little over two and a half miles."

"Then, when they get to the cabin," she continued, "Wolff starts taking care of him. He breaks up the furniture to start a fire, he melts snow in that kettle, and then he goes out to chop more wood."

"That's what the forensic team reported as having happened, yes," Buzz confirmed. "But then they leave the cabin. Why? That's the part that doesn't make sense."

"It's obvious to me," she answered, "that they didn't leave

of their own free will. Rick Wolff can be a wildman some-times, but he is *not* crazy. They had everything they needed to survive for well over a week, but then they just get up and leave. If they weren't captured, then you tell me what happened."

Buzz clenched his fists. "For Christ's sake, Ruby, I don't know. Maybe Wolff was hurt too and was out of his head. I just don't fucking know."

"If Wolff had also been hurt," Ruby pointed out, "he wouldn't have been able to carry Mojo as far as that cabin. And," she pressed her point, "we still haven't talked about why they went down in the first place. From what I've heard through rumor control, all the electronic circuits in the ship were burned out."

"Red talks too fucking much," Buzz snapped.

Ruby ignored him and continued. "And why haven't we been able to pick up their personal location beacons? They're supposed to be good for two weeks, aren't they?"

Buzz nodded.

"It looks to me like whatever burned out the Griffin's elec-tronics got their locators as well. And," Mom pressed her point even harder, "just what in the world is powerful enough to do that?"

"Maybe they got hit by lightning?"

"Bullshit," Mom snorted. "You're a pilot, Buzz. You know better than that. Aircraft get hit by lightning all the time and the engines still keep running."

Buzz locked eyes with her. "How do you know that the turbines were shut down when they hit the ground? That's supposed to be classified."

Mom looked as innocent as a teenage virgin. "I have my sources too."

"I'm going to kick Red's ass up between his fucking ears," Buzz said in exasperation. He turned away and started pac-ing impatiently. "How in the hell can I run an investigation if everything gets leaked as soon as . . ."

147

"But you're not running an investigation," Mom pointed out as she watched Buzz carefully. "You're packing everything up and running home with your tail between your legs like a whipped dog."

Now Buzz was mad. "God damn it, Ruby, I don't have to take that shit from you. We've been called home and we fucking well are going to *go* home."

Mom leaned back in her chair and smiled as she slowly looked her commanding officer up and down.

"Good boy," she said. "You go home just like you've been told to do. Don't let a little thing like having two of your best officers being held captive somewhere get in the way of following orders. After all, Mojo and the Wolfman would do the same thing if they were in your shoes. They wouldn't lift a finger to help you if they were ordered to go home. They'd go back like good little boys and leave your ass hanging in the wind." She shrugged. "So why shouldn't you do the same to them?"

For a moment Mom thought that Buzz was going to explode. His face got redder and redder, his fists clenched, and he stopped breathing. She thought that she had finally gone too far.

"God damn you," he said softly. "God damn that smart mouth of yours. Just who in the hell do you think you are to talk to me that way? I've done more to get those two fuckheads out of jams than anyone in this force, I've put my career on the line time after time to keep them from . . ."

"Then why aren't you out there doing it this time?" She stood up to face him. "They're really in bad trouble this time and you're just going to pack it up and go home. Why? God damn it, J.D.," she stabbed him in the chest with her finger. "You tell me why."

Buzz stopped like he had been slapped in the face. No one called him J.D. No one! He hated that name. Now he really did explode. "Sergeant Jenkins, You are way out of line, and I'm not going to listen to any more of this shit

148

from you. You have your orders. You carry them out or you're going to find yourself written up on charges of insubordination."

Mom looked at Buzz with a unreadable expression on her face. She slowly took her headset off and laid it back down on the console. Next she unpinned her TPF sergeant's badge and placed it next to the headset.

"I'm past minimum retirement age," she said softly. "And I just retired. I will accept a ride back to Denver, as is provided in the regulations when a retirement occurs away from a permanent duty station."

Buzz stood there with his mouth open. "But, Ruby, you can't do that."

"I just did, asshole," she flared up. "And now that I'm a citizen again and not a cop, you're not my commander anymore and I've got a few things to say to you . . ."

Several meters away from the CP tent, Red smiled around the stub of the cigar clenched tightly between his teeth. He had been headed into the tent to have a word with Buzz when he heard the argument between Mom and Buzz start to heat up. Wisely, he had stopped, still within earshot however, and listened to the verbal fireworks.

Buzz thought that he was a badass, but there was no one in the entire Tac Force who could hold a candle to Ruby Jenkins when she got up a good head of steam. Red liked to think that he was bad enough to hold his own against all comers too, but even he knew better than to cross swords with Mom. Not if he wanted to come out of it with his manhood still intact. That old bitch had a heart of stainless steel and a mouth that spit pure sulfuric acid.

"What do we do now, Red?" one of the packing crew asked. Mom could be heard all over the airfield as she took a strip off Buzz's ass.

Red shifted the cigar to the other side of his mouth, spit a

149

thin stream of tobacco juice into the snow, and smiled. "I'd just kind of hold tight for now," he said. "Look busy, but don't pack anything else up."

"Yes, sir," the man smiled knowingly. Mom wasn't the only one who felt badly about not having found Wolff and Mojo. As cold and as miserable as it was on this godforsaken mountain airstrip, every man and woman in Dragon Flight had busted their ass to do what they could for the operation. Mom might not be aware of it, but everyone within earshot was silently cheering for her.

Zoomie walked up to Red with a big grin on his face. "Makes me feel homesick," he said. "My mother used to discuss things with Dad that way. Us kids used to hide upstairs until the fallout passed."

Zumwald was closer to the truth than he realized when he likened Mom and Buzz's argument to a marital fight, but he had no way of knowing it. Red was probably the only person in Dragon Flight who knew that in the early days Ruby and Buzz had tangled in the sheets more than once. But their relationship had been doomed to failure from the very start. Both of them were just too damned independent to give in enough to make it work.

Neither one of them had ever let their personal lives get in the way of doing their duties, however, and they usually worked well together. But the battle today had turned out to be more than just a difference of opinion over what to do about the two missing officers. It had drifted over into the forbidden realm of personalities.

Just then they both heard Buzz bellow something about Mom being a pigheaded, foul-mouthed, dried-up old bitch. Red winced and clamped down on his cigar. Buzz had just made a critical error in judgement. Now the shit was *really* going to hit the fan.

You could say damned near anything to Mom that you wanted; she never held grudges for something said in anger. But it was not wise to remind her of her age. Anyone foolish enough to do that was lucky to be able to crawl away afterward, bleeding and broken.

Red threw his arm over Zoomie's shoulders. "What say you and I see go if there's any of my coffee left, son," he said in a rare fatherly tone. "It's not nice to listen in on a private command discussion. Not good form, what?"

Zoomie laughed. "Right."

Chapter Nineteen

Caesar's Palace was ablaze with light and noise on New Year's Eve. Swarms of revelers crowded the gaming tables and slot machines, and the hotel had put on a free champagne buffet on the rear patio by the pool. Food and drink and party hats were free to all comers on a night that came only every thousand years. It was costing the hotel millions to host this party, but it could all be written off as public relations, so it was full speed ahead. Even the Roman emperors the casino was named after could not have done a better job of throwing a party.

In the plush penthouse apartment on the casino's top floor, Buck Sloan wore a practiced smile as he shook the hands of dozens of well-wishers at his own private party. This was a black-tie, invitation-only affair, and the guest list consisted of the elite of the Sun Belt's political, entertainment, and moneyed circles. This party too was costing Sloan a mint, but he was writing it off as a campaign expense. So unlike the cheap stuff that was being served downstairs, only vintage champagne flowed in the penthouse. No wonder that it cost so much to run for president.

Mattiese was frantically trying to get his boss to stay in

152

one place long enough so he could introduce him to all of the VIPs and not so VIPs who wanted to meet the next president of the United States. This was the part that Sloan hated the most about politics, but he knew that this was the single most important element of his campaign. Sloan's power in the polls came from the true believers, the common people, but the guests at his party had enough money and influence to get a baboon elected president if the mood struck them. They could also *keep* him from being elected if they wanted too, so he needed to have this moneyed elite firmly in his camp along with the ordinary voters.

Sloan didn't give a shit that most of them couldn't even spell *environmentalist*, and he was fully aware that most of them couldn't care less about the environmental platform of his Clean Earth party. They supported him because they saw him as one of their own rather than merely another mediocre East Coast political hack. They also saw their own personal fortunes rising if Sloan were to be elected, and they all wanted their own piece of the plump pie that they saw coming after his inauguration.

Sloan knew all of this, and that was why he had the practiced smile plastered on his face. He quickly glanced down at his watch to see how much more of this he had to endure before he could make good his escape.

"Oh, Buck?"

He turned to see a middle-aged woman standing at his side. She was tastefully dressed in a modest five-thousand-dollar smock, and the fingers of the manicured hand she held out to him had at least twenty carats on them. "I just want to tell you how badly I feel about those poor kids who were arrested in the national forest," the woman gushed.

He put on his serious face as he took her hand. "Yes," he said slowly, launching into the statement that Mattiese had prepared for him on the topic. "That was just one more example of the excesses we have seen lately from the Tactical Police Force. I firmly believe that every American citizen has a right to demonstrate for those things that he holds most dear."

His voice took on a stronger tone. "And this is one thing that my administration will fight for—the basic right of the people of this great nation to peacefully protest."

"I would like to make a small donation to help those poor kids," the woman said, opening a small, diamond-studded purse, "Maybe to help with their defense costs or something like that." The woman folded up several hundred-dollar bills and held them out to him.

"Thank you," Buck said as he took her arm and steered her toward Mattiese. "He can give you a receipt for this."

"Oh! That isn't necessary," the woman gushed. "I trust you."

Buck smiled to himself. "The Presidential Election Commission likes to see receipts," he explained. "They don't believe in trust."

Passing the woman off to his campaign manager, Buck went back to shaking hands and making small talk.

At the Forest Service airstrip, Red had gotten quite a party going in the maintenance tent. The maintenance chief was always ready for a party, and even being stuck way the hell out in the woods was not going to stop him when there was something special to celebrate. After all, this was New Year's Eve, 1999. It would be a thousand years before this particular reason for a party came around again, and he was sure as hell not going to miss it.

Being out in the woods made having a party a little more difficult, but not impossible—not for a man of Red's resources. After Buzz had issued the orders that they would extend the search in the forest for three more days, Red made his plan and sprang into action. It had been easy to send two of the Griffins to the closest town, Grimsley, Colorado, on a maintenance test flight.

The fact that the choppers had landed right next door to the town's liquor store had merely been a fortuitous coincidence. So had been the fact that the air crews had been loaded down with every dollar bill that anyone had on them.

As a result, upon returning to the airstrip, the Griffins had been loaded down with goodies to eat and drink. While the choppers had been gone, Red had supervised turning the maintenance tent into an open-air party room. He had even hauled over one of the extra generators to run additional radiant heaters so the beer wouldn't freeze. Ice was not going to be a problem at this party.

Since everyone had been on stand-down since the last flight, the party started as soon as the tent was set up. One of the things that had come back on the Griffins was almost a hundred pounds of sirloin steak and several bags of charcoal. Within fifteen minutes the chief cook from the mess was busily grilling them to order over charcoal pits dug deep into the frozen ground, while the rest of the cooks whipped up the fixings to go with them.

By the time that the first of the steaks were done, everyone was in a party mood. And with the extension of the search, they had good reason to celebrate. Even if Mojo and the Wolfman were still wandering around somewhere out there in the cold, the Tac Force was convinced that they would be recovered alive. They were confident that something would break in the morning.

As soon as everyone had gotten something to eat, the mess crew broke up their operation and joined in the festivities themselves. The dirty dishes could wait until the morning. The way things were going there would be few takers for breakfast anyway.

As the midnight hour approached, Zumwald climbed up on one of the tables, a hand-held bullhorn in one hand, a bottle of Coors in the other. He held the bullhorn up to his mouth and switched it on.

"Testing, one, two," his amplified voice blasted through the tent. People yelled and clapped their hands over their ears.

"Too loud?" he asked, dodging the plastic cup of beer that someone threw at him. He turned the volume down and tried it again. "Testing, testing."

When no one complained, he knew that he had the volume right. "Okay, okay," he said. "Let's hold it down here for a moment."

"Up yours, Zumwald!" someone shouted.

"Don't you wish," Zoomie grinned. "Okay, boys and girls, it's just about that time." He glanced down at his watch. "Everyone get ready."

"And for those of you who are so inclined, the rules against fraternizing on duty hours will be suspended for the next half hour."

"But we're not on duty!" someone shouted.

"A minor point," Zoomie answered. "But be careful of who you try to fraternize with. Red gets a little touchy about stuff like that."

The maintenance chief shot him the finger from the other side of the tent.

"Okay!" Zoomie shouted "Here it comes! Five, Four, Three, Two, One! Happy New Year!"

The tent broke out in happy shouts as Dragon Flight welcomed in the year 2000.

As the crowd roared and cheered, Buzz looked around the tent for Mom, but he didn't see her anywhere. He looked out at the airstrip and saw a solitary figure standing over by the nose of one of the Griffins. From the figure's small size, he knew that it had to be either Mom or one of Dragon Flight's other female officers, but he was betting that it was Ruby. He got another bottle of Coors from the beer trailer and walked out to her.

"Ruby," he said, twisting the top off the bottle as he walked up behind her. "I brought you a refill."

Mom spun around at the sound of his voice. "What in the hell are you doing here, Buzz?"

He held the bottle out. "I brought you a beer."

She stared at him for a moment before reaching out and taking the bottle. "Thanks," she said gruffly.

"No sweat," he said. "Happy New Year."

They stood in silence for the next few moments. "I wonder where they are right now," Buzz broke the silence.

"Damn you, Buzz Corcran," Mom said, her defenses going up instantly. "Don't start that again."

"Wait a minute," he said softly, holding up his hand. "I'm just trying to apologize for some of the things I said this afternoon. I was way out of line, and I want to say that I'm sorry."

Mom turned to look at him. "You old bastard," she said. "Don't you go getting soft on me now."

"No," he said. "I mean it. I'm sorry for most of what I said this afternoon."

"Not for all of it?" she smiled.

Buzz thought for a moment. "No," he said slowly, "some of it was right on."

"Like what, for instance?"

Buzz grinned. "Oh," he said, "the part where I said that you were a loudmouthed old biddy."

"You're going to get your ass kicked if you're not careful, Buzz Corcran."

"Hey, wait a minute," he said, backing off a step. "I'm trying to say that I'm sorry."

"That's not what it sounds like to me."

"I am, Ruby, believe me, I am," Buzz tried to sound sincere. "I really want you to take your badge back and help me find those two boys."

"We'll find them," she promised. "We'll find them if it takes us all week."

"We've only got three more days," he reminded her. "And then we really do have to go back to work. I used up a lifetime of favors to get us this extension, and I won't be able to push it any farther. If we don't find something in these next three days, we've got to pack it up."

She looked out at the cold, snow-covered mountains in the distance. "I know," she said softly. "But I also know that they're out there somewhere. We just have to find them."

As soon as the clock struck midnight, Buck Sloan shook a few more hands and slipped away from the crowd while they sang "Auld Lang Syne." By this time everyone was so wasted that they were unlikely to notice that their host had vanished.

His chauffeur picked him up at the back of the casino and drove him to the Las Vegas general aviation airport at the edge of the town. His personal jet was waiting for him on the tarmac, its turbines turning over at an idle as he climbed into the copilot's seat and buckled in for the flight to the airstrip right outside Medicine Bow National Forest in Wyoming. From there he would take a chopper to his hidden satellite communications facility inside Medicine Mountain.

After construction at the site had been completed and all the equipment installed, he had spent very little time there so as not to have to explain long absences. But while he was satisfied to let his technicians run the routine satellite communications intercepts, this was one event that he wanted to supervise in person.

His New Dawn project was the culmination of months of careful planning, and it had cost him millions of his own dollars, to say nothing of the billions the Family had given him. It was only natural that he would want to be on hand to witness its implementation.

As soon as the pilot lifted off the runway and tucked the

plane's gear up, Sloan leaned back to take a short nap. There was still a great deal to do tonight and he wanted to be fresh when he destroyed California's Diablo Canyon nuclear power plant in the morning.

Chapter Twenty

Medicine Mountain; 1 January 2000

Dawn of New Year's Day 2000 broke clear over Medicine Bow National Forest. A brilliant sun glittered off the snow-covered mountains and the sky was a deep china blue. It was a perfect day to start a new millennium.

In the rest of the world, however, things were not going so well. Fanatical religious leaders of every stripe had taken this opportunity to bring destruction to their enemies, both real and imagined. The faithful had worked themselves into mystical frenzies and had wreaked widespread devastation in the names of their gods and their prophets.

Over a million were reported dead in India alone and war raged along the border with Pakistan. The body count in the Middle East would take weeks to sort out, but most of the casualties were Muslim and Russian. After the short but devastating Arab-Israeli war of 1992, no one was willing to take the Iraelis on again, no matter what. Even Western Europe was counting its dead. The Vatican was in rubble and it was rumored that the pope had been killed in the rioting caused by a vision of the Virgin Mary seen by hundreds of thousands of worshipers.

In the New World, a charismatic Mexican priest led thousands of his followers to their watery deaths in the

Gulf of Mexico. He had promised them that on this day they could walk to the Holy Land to meet Jesus. The Native American populations of several Latin American countries had risen to throw off what they saw as their Spanish oppressors, and the blood ran deep. In Peru, an Indian proclaimed himself the new Inca and gathered thousands for a raid on Lima.

The United States of America had not been spared this particular form of mass insanity either. Junkies OD'ed, rioters burned large areas of the northeastern urban slums, and downtown LA resembled a post-Holocaust war zone as black and Hispanic gangs warred.

All over the nation, New Agers, the faithful, and Christian fundamentalists alike died violently in the name of peace, love, and the coming of the new millennium. Mass suicides were common, and of the ten thousand people packed into the Brotherly Love Covenant for a pray-in to protect the nation against the coming of the Antichrist, only a few hundred survived when the flashy TV cathedral was torched.

It was as if every thousand years humanity needed to purge itself with an orgy of murder and mass destruction. The beginning of this millennium was no different than the last. In the aftermath of the year 2000, it would take months before life on the planet returned to normal.

In the mountains of the Medicine Bow National Forest, however, none of this turmoil was evident. The only sign of activity in the forest was deep within Medicine Mountain, far from prying eyes.

In Sloan's satellite communications control room, the technicians were preparing for Operation New Dawn. In a few hours, one of the air force's laser-armed SDI missile-killer satellites would be in position over the coast of Southern California. Once it was in position, Sloan's people would take control of it and retarget the laser weapon on board.

Operating in the cold vacuum of space, this laser-equipped satellite was America's first line of defense against the greatest threat of the late twentieth century—nuclear missiles in the hands of Third World nations. With the end of the Cold War in the early nineties, the United States and the Soviet Union had scrapped almost all of their nuclear weapons. Arms control had come too late, however, to prevent the proliferation of nuclear technology to other nations, nations less able to control their use.

The short but devastating Arab-Israeli war of 1992 saw the first use of tactical nuclear weapons since the end of World War II when the Syrians launched one of their nuclear-tipped rockets at Tel Aviv. No one ever knew for certain if the missile had been launched on orders of the Syrian leaders or by accident, but regardless of the reason the Israelis instantly retaliated with their own nuclear weapons.

When the war ended the next day, Libya, Iran, Syria, Egypt, and the Palestinians had been destroyed as military powers for the next hundred years. Regardless of that, however, nuclear weapons remained in the hands of other equally irresponsible nations, and the threat of yet another nuclear war continued.

In response to this threat, both the United States and the Soviet Union rushed to develop killer satellites. In the United States, the old plans for the Strategic Defense Initiative first promoted during the Reagan administration were quickly put into production, and missile-killer satellites were launched into orbit. The lasers on these satellites were powerful enough to destroy enemy nuclear missiles still on their launch pads in Asia and the Middle East.

These purely defensive weapons had been designed to protect America against enemy nuclear weapons, but this time one of them would be aimed at a target inside the

United States—the nuclear power facility at Diablo Canyon, California.

Once the weapon was zeroed in on the nuclear fuel containment building at the power plant, it would take only seconds for the laser's beam to burn through the protective layers of concrete and cause a nuclear meltdown at the facility. The resulting explosion would contaminate a large area of both California and the Pacific Ocean. The disaster would make the Chernoble meltdown look like a minor inconvenience in comparison.

And since all traces of the cause of the meltdown would be lost in the rubble, it would appear as if the feared nuclear disaster that the antinuke environmentalists had been screaming about for decades had finally occurred. The protests would begin immediately.

The result of Sloan's plan would be that the United States would immediately outlaw all nuclear facilities. With the current antipathy to oil and coal, the only thing that could replace them would be the SOLCO-built solar power facilities. Since Sloan owned not only the patents on this expensive energy system but the manufacturing facilities to produce them as well, he would soon become a very wealthy man, not to mention the next president of the United States.

The SDI killer satellites had been designed to be immune from this kind of hostile takeover. But these protections were all electronic, and anything that is electronic can be bypassed, particularly by someone who had Sloan's kind of money. The money had not only paid for the secret satellite communications facility buried deep in the mountain, it had also bought the highly classified SDI satellite security codes needed to make the satellite accept maneuvering instructions. A disgruntled defense industry scientist who had been dismissed from his top secret SDI duties for homosexual activity had been glad to hand them over . . . for a tidy sum.

In a few short hours, a New Dawn would bloom over the coast of Southern California, but it would not be a dawn of clear skies and the hope for peace in the new millennium. It would be the dawn of a nuclear disaster unprecedented in the history of mankind.

At the Forest Service airstrip, the men and women of Dragon Flight rose to meet the dawn. Even though most of them had tried to be careful the night before, there were still a few hangovers that had to be nursed before their owners could operate at a hundred percent. But as always, Red Larson was on hand to kick ass and take the names of anyone who wasn't moving fast enough, and that helped people forget their alcohol-induced miseries.

Red showed no visible signs that he too had gotten a little too close to his bottle of Jack Daniels. A throbbing headache, however, reminded him that he was getting a little too old to celebrate that much. But it didn't slow him down. If anything, it gave him a good reason to focus on what was going on this morning. He was in fine form as he went from one man to the next, making sure that he was doing what Red thought he should be doing.

He quietly walked up behind one of his mechanics, who was hammering on a box-end wrench trying to loosen a stubborn nut. He shifted the stub of his cigar to the other side of his mouth as he leaned over the man. "Just exactly what do you think you're doing?" Red yelled in his ear.

The mechanic jumped to his feet, the hammer falling from his hand. "Ah . . . the nut was frozen," he said.

"So you were pounding on it with a hammer," Red smiled.

The man nodded. "It was frozen, Chief, and I thought . . ."

"It was frozen, so you were pounding on it?"

"Yes, sir."

"If I ever catch you pounding on anything other than your pud," Red yelled in his face, "I'm going to pound on you with a baseball bat! If it's frozen, you fucking heat it! You do *not* pound on my helicopters with a fucking hammer."

The man staggered back two steps. "Yes, sir."

"Jesus," Red muttered as he walked away chomping on his cigar. He'd be glad when they found those two cowboys so he could get this operation back to Denver and his heated hangers. Trying to fix things in the snow wasn't cutting it.

"Yo! Dickhead!" he yelled at a man who was spilling turbine oil down the side of one of the ships as he topped off the oil tank.

The mechanic nearest him turned around, terror in his eyes. "Not you," Red spat, "I was talking to that other dickhead."

While Red was verbally abusing the support troops outside, Buzz was holding an aircrew meeting inside the big tent. Some of the flyers were a little under the weather as well, so Buzz kept it short and to the point.

"Okay, people," he said. "Here it is. We've only got three days and every minute has got to count. Wolff and Mugabe have been down for a week now, and the experts say that they could still be alive if they got into cover of some kind. But the experts also say that unless they've been able to catch something to eat, they will be at the extreme limits of survival in this kind of weather by now. Therefore, this is the last chance, both theirs and ours, and every last minute counts."

"To get maximum coverage of the search area, I want you down on the deck and checking out anything that looks out of place. Everyone will be tac linked back to here and I want constant reports on everything you're seeing. Believe me, no one is going to get chewed out if they stop and take a closer look at something. The object of the exercise for the next three days is not only to cover a lot of ground, but to do it thoroughly and not to miss a thing."

He looked over at Jack Zumwald. "Zoomie, I want you to break your people up and send a squad in each of the Griffins along with one snowmobile. If need be, work your people on the ground while the choppers spot for them."

"No problem, sir," The platoon leader answered. "It'll probably work better that way."

"The CP will be operating twenty-four hours a day, so I expect you to keep flying until you can't fly anymore. The weather people say that the next storm isn't due to pass through here until the end of this three-day period, so that won't be getting in our road."

Buzz looked around the room. "Are there any questions?"

"If there are none, get to your ships, get out there, and find those guys."

The tent cleared instantly.

Outside, Zoomie caught up with Gunner and Legs. "I'll be going with you guys again," he told them.

"Better get a hustle on it," Gunner said, when he saw that the Tac cop didn't have all his gear with him. "I'm cranking her up as soon as I can."

"Don't worry," Zoomie said, spinning around. "I'll be there as soon as I get my stuff."

Deep inside the mountain, Mugabe stirred awake and sat up. "Happy fucking New Year," Wolff greeted him. "Welcome to the new millennium."

"Right," Mugabe grimaced as he tried to move his left arm.

"How's it feeling?" Wolff's concern was plain in his voice.

"It's not as bad as it was," the gunner said, "but it's still not up to a hundred percent."

"Good," the pilot said, "because I think it's about time that you and I got the fuck outta here."

"What in the hell are you talking about?" Mugabe frowned. "In case you haven't checked lately, we're still being held prisoner inside a mountain."

"That thought had occurred to me," Wolff admitted, "But there's something going on out there today. I thought I heard a chopper fly in late last night, and I've heard a lot of people running up and down the hallway."

"So?"

"Well," Wolff grinned. "I was thinking that if there is something special going down today, this just might be a real good time for us to break out of here and kind of disappear in the crowd. Maybe find us a way out of here and fade back into the underbrush."

"And just how in the hell do you plan to do that?" Mojo said. "Have you been holding out on me? You've got a satchel charge hidden away that you haven't told me about?"

"There was this thing I saw in a movie once," Wolff looked up at the ceiling of the small cell. "And I've always wanted to give it a try."

"Oh, shit!" Mojo said, shaking his head. "Another one of your fucking stunts."

Wolff grinned. "Believe me, you're going to love this one."

"Don't keep me in suspense. What is it?"

"It's like this," Wolff explained. "There was this movie and the hero was stuck in a cell like this and couldn't get out. So, he . . ." Wolff laid out his plan.

When Wolff was done, Mojo just sat and stared at him. "You're fucking nuts," he shook his head. "You know that, don't you? You've been in here too long; the confinement has turned your brains into Silly Putty."

"You got a better idea?" Wolff was suddenly very serious.

"No."

"Then what do we have to lose?" Wolff asked. "All they can do is shoot me, and they're going to kill us anyway. If we're ever going to get out of here, we'd better take the chance while we still can."

"There is that," Mojo agreed. "Okay, let's do it."

Chapter Twenty-one

Medicine Mountain; 1 January

Mojo hammered his good hand on the steel door to the cell. "Guard!" he yelled. "Guard!"

When he finally heard the hammering of feet running down the hall, he started pounding even harder. "Hey! Guard! Get over here!"

The guard fumbled with the lock on the cell door. "What the hell's going on in there?" he shouted through the door.

"Where's my partner?" Mojo yelled back. "What have you done with him?"

"What the fuck are you talking about?" The guard struggled to get the lock off and the door open. "He'd better be in there with you."

"I'm telling you he ain't here," Mojo answered. "I woke up and he was gone."

His pistol drawn, the man quickly stepped into the room. He stopped abruptly right inside the doorway when he saw that Mojo was in fact standing there all by himself. "Where'd he go!?"

Before the guard could recover from his surprise, Wolff dropped down from where he had been holding himself up with his back to the ceiling, his hands and feet braced against the walls like a mountain climber. He landed on the guard's back, driving the man down to his hands and

169

knees. Before the guard could recover, Wolff linked the fingers of both hands together and hammered his doubled fist down against the base of his skull. The guard's spine snapped with the blow and he flopped forward onto his face.

Mojo was on him in an instant, but his body was completely limp. "I think you killed him," he said, checking his neck for a pulse.

"Tough shit," Wolff said, reaching down to scoop up the guard's pistol. "Let's get outta here. Someone might have heard you yelling."

"Wait!" Mugabe said. "Get his uniform."

"Good idea."

Wolff quickly stripped the guard and stepped into his blue coveralls. Zipping them up over his flight suit, he also buckled the man's pistol belt around his waist. "What do we do with him?"

"Put him on your cot under the blanket," Mojo said as he tried to make his own cot look like there was someone sleeping in it. "So he'll look like you."

A few seconds later the guard was laid out with his back to the door and the blanket pulled up around his neck. At a cursory glance, he would pass for Wolff. Hopefully no one would miss the guard and come looking for him.

"Let's get the hell outta here," Wolff said, the guard's pistol at the ready as he cautiously peered around the edge of the open door to see if anyone was in the hallway.

It was clear, and as the two men slipped out in the hall. Wolff pulled the door shut behind him, slipped the padlock back through the hasp, and locked it again. "Which way?" he whispered.

Mojo quickly looked up and down the hall. "This way," he said, pointing away from the route they had taken to their cell several days ago.

Mugabe led the way while Wolff brought up the rear

holding the pistol on him. If anyone spotted them, the pilot hoped that they wouldn't look any further than the stolen uniform and think that Mojo was being escorted somewhere for interrogation.

As they rounded the first corner, two men approached them going the other way, but with Wolff's coveralls, a week's worth of beard, and the pistol, neither one paid any attention to them. Mugabe kept navigating for them, making his decisions purely by instinct until they came to a door with a sign on it reading "Turn all lights off before opening."

"That's got to be the way out," Wolff said when he spotted a row of thick, fur-lined parkas hanging on a rack by the door.

The two cops quickly donned parkas and pulled the hoods up to cover their faces before they opened the door.

In the central control room of the hidden mountain facility, Sloan and his technicians were completing their preparations to implement New Dawn. The command communication channels to the killer satellite had been thoroughly tested, and the targeting data needed to aim the laser weapon at the nuclear power plant had been computed and was ready to transmit.

If Sloan's plan was going to work, split-second timing was absolutely essential. Even though he had the security codes to control the satellite, there was still one thing he was not one hundred percent certain about. The killer birds had a fail-safe system built into them, and he was not certain that he could override it for more than a few seconds. As soon as the Aerospace Command trackers noticed that one of their laser-armed satellites had altered its programmed flight path, a command to self-destruct would be immediately transmitted up to it.

To confuse the aerospace satellite controllers, Sloan was

171

planning to send a false signal on the satellite's frequency pattern relaying information indicating that the bird was still where it was supposed to be in its orbit. By bouncing the phony signal off a standard communications relay satellite, the data would appear to have originated from deep space, not from a radio on earth.

This would buy him valuable time by confusing the air force for a while and forcing them to double-check their data through a radar tracking station. This procedure would take a few precious minutes. While they were doing that, Sloan would be free to fire the laser.

Once the laser had burned through the nuclear containment building at the power plant, he would turn control of the satellite back to the air force and no one would ever be able to prove that it had been taken over for those critical few minutes.

Wolff squinted and shielded his eyes from the bright glare of the sun against the snow. After the long days spent in the dimly lighted cell, it took time for his eyes to adjust to the sunlight. When he could see, he found that they were in a protected hollow against the side of the mountain. Huge boulders ringed an area about the size of a football field, creating a flat clearing. With the deep snow covering it, Wolff couldn't tell if the clearing was a natural formation or something that had been created along with the underground facility.

Wolff was betting that it was man-made, however, like everything else he had seen under the mountain so far. The door they had exited from was camouflaged to look like another rock, and when it was closed it would be almost impossible to spot from the air.

Mojo peered around the corner of the boulder half covering the entrance. "Wolff!" he pointed to the far edge of the clearing. "There's a chopper over there!"

172

Wolff snapped his head around and spotted the sleek, small shape of a four-place Bell executive ship sitting out in the open. "Let's go!" he whispered hoarsely, grabbing Mojo by the arm. "That's our ticket out of this fucking place."

The two cops raced across the snow-covered ground, their eyes darting from side to side as they ran. They skidded to a halt under cover behind the chopper. After checking to make sure that they were alone, Wolff opened the right-hand door and slid into the pilot's seat. Mojo scrambled up into the copilot's side and buckled the shoulder harness.

"You think you can fly this thing?" the gunner whispered.

"Does a bear shit in the woods?" Wolff whispered back, a big grin on his face as he placed his feet on the rudder pedals. "Of course I can fly this fucking thing, it has rotors doesn't it?"

Wolff took a moment to study the unfamiliar controls before he started flipping switches on the instrument panel. When the power finally came on, he energized the starter and triggered the turbine ignition switch. The turbine ignited with a whoosh, and the rotor blades slowly began to turn over their heads.

The warm smell of burning kerosene wafted into the cockpit as Wolff kept the turbine RPMs down to flight idle until the blades came up to speed. "Come on! Come on!" he muttered, his eyes fixed on the rotor's tachometer.

As soon as the needle reached the green zone, he twisted the throttle up against the stop. When the whine of the turbine built to a scream and the needle snapped over to the edge of the red line, Wolff hauled sharply up on the collective. The small chopper leaped from the ground like it had been shot out of a cannon.

As soon as the chopper's skids cleared the boulders surrounding the hollow, Wolff slammed the cyclic over against the right-hand stop, throwing the ship into a hard bank only a few feet above the ground. He snapped out of the turn and shoved her nose down to gain air speed as she raced down the side of the mountain.

"Get on the emergency channel, Mojo, and see if anyone's out there looking for us."

The gunner quickly switched the VHF radio over to Guard, the emergency channel, and keyed the mike. "Any station, any station, Mayday! Mayday! This is Mojo and the Wolfman. Come in, please."

He released the transmission switch and listened for a few seconds before keying the mike again. "Any station, any station, Mayday! Mayday! Mayday! This is Dragon Lead calling any station."

"Keep trying!" Wolff shouted. "They've got to be out there somewhere."

"Mayday! Mayday! This is Dragon Lead, come in."

In the central control room, Sloan's radar operator picked up the blip of the stolen helicopter as soon as it left the enclosure. "Buck!" he yelled across the room, "someone's taking your chopper up!"

Sloan jumped up from his seat and punched on the screens for the optical scanners on the mountain. They showed the small white Bell ship racing down the slope, headed for the forest below. "Stop those fuckers!" he yelled to the man on the weapons console.

The all-white paint job on the stolen chopper made it difficult to spot against the harsh glare of the snow, but that would not prevent the EMP weapon's targeting radar from finding it.

The door in the side of the mountain slid open and the dish antenna mounted on the antiaircraft gun chassis appeared in the opening. The dish tracked the small chopper for several seconds, moving swiftly as it followed

Wolff's wildly maneuvering machine all over the sky. A hundred meters before the chopper reached the safety of the tree line, the targeting radar got a lock-on.

The dish hummed deeply for several seconds, tracked the chopper again, and hummed once more.

In the cockpit of the fleeing Bell the whine of the turbine and the radios both went dead at the same time. The controls went stiff in Wolff's hands as the turbine-powered hydraulic system cut out too. "Hang on!" the pilot shouted. "We've lost control!"

This time, however, since the helicopter had just been skimming over the ground, Wolff couldn't even begin to try to autorotate. All he could do was ride the machine down to a crash landing. But at least they didn't have far to fall when the chopper crashed.

The small ship skidded along on top of the snow for a few meters. Wolff fought to keep it level, but one skid hit a boulder and dipped over to one side. The still-spinning rotor blades caught in the snow and shattered. The nose dug into the snow and the tail boom came over the top, shoving the cockpit into the ground. The tail boom snapped off, but not before its momentum threw the chopper back upright. They came to rest against a snowbank lying on the left side.

For a moment neither of them moved, stunned by the crash. "You okay?" Wolff asked.

"Yeah," Mojo grunted as he fumbled for his harness release with his good hand. "Let's get outta here 'fore this sucker blows up."

The two men crawled out of the wreckage and staggered a short distance away from the downed ship. "Jesus, Wolfman," Mojo said softly, "I thought you said you could fly this thing."

"The power cut out," Wolff answered, rubbing his shoulder where he had been thrown against the harness. "Just like on the Griffin."

175

They both heard the faint sound of racing engines and looked back up the slope of the mountain. Three snowmobiles, each carrying two men, were racing down the side of the mountain toward them. The pilot could see that they had weapons in their hands. There was no way that they were going to get away from them.

"Ah, shit," he muttered, slowly raising his hands high up over his head. "Here we go again."

Chapter Twenty-two

Medicine Mountain; 1 January

In the valley below the mountain, One Two had dropped off its search team to sweep a small wooded area while the chopper checked out a different location. This section of the forest had already been searched, but the team was double-checking in case anything had been missed the first time around. The four men were working their way through the woods, heading up the side of the mountain, when one of the men caught a fleeting glimpse of the stolen chopper through the tall trees.

"Hey!" he shouted over to his team leader. "I think I just saw a chopper and it's sure as hell not one of ours."

"Where?"

The Tac cop turned back to look again, but saw nothing. Where in the hell had it gone? "It was right over there just a second ago," he pointed to the left of the mountain. "Maybe fifteen hundred meters out and moving to the west. It wasn't one of ours 'cause it was painted white."

"Better call it in," the team leader said. "Buzz said he want's to hear about anything we see."

The man who had spotted the ship switched over to the command frequency and keyed his mike, "Dragon Control, this is Tac Two Bravo."

"This is Control," came Mom's voice. "Go ahead."

"This is Tac Two. I think I may have spotted something."

No one had answered Mojo's call for help when he had been broadcasting on the emergency channel, but it had not gone unheeded. The transmission had been picked up by the Guard channel receiver on Mom's commo console and automatically recorded. A red light on the face of the receiver started blinking to indicate that an emergency message had been recorded and was waiting to be played back.

Mom had been in communication with one of the Griffins when the message had come in, and she had not noticed the call light come on. When she did see it blinking, she instantly reached over and hit the message playback button. Mugabe's voice filled her earphones. "Any station, any station, Mayday! Mayday! This is Mojo and the Wolfman. Come in, please."

Mom came straight out of her chair as if she'd been shot. "Buzz!" she shouted. "We've found them!"

Buzz came streaking over to the commo console, his face tense. "Where?"

"Listen," Mom said, playing back the distress call over the loudspeaker so Buzz could hear it as she keyed her throat mike. "Dragon Lead, Dragon Lead, this is Dragon Control answering your Mayday. Come in."

When there was no immediate answer, she tried again. "Wolff, Mojo, this is Control. Come in, please."

While Mom continued to try to make contact, Buzz listened to the recorded emergency message again. He could detect a faint rhythmic vibration in the transmission, as if Mugabe was speaking over a chopper radio in flight. The third, and last, call from Mojo had been cut off abruptly in mid-sentence. It sounded as if the radio had gone dead or the chopper they were calling from had crashed.

"Where'd that call come from?" Buzz snapped.

Mom read the three-digit number giving the compass bearing to the original radio transmission.

"That's over in the direction of the mountain," Buzz said, glancing at the map.

Just then, One Two's search team called in with their possible sighting of an unidentified chopper in the same general area.

Buzz made his decision in a flash. Mojo must have been in a chopper and it had gone down the same way that the Griffin had gone down. "Get Zoomie's people up there fast," he ordered. "All of them."

"I told you they were alive."

Buzz didn't change expression. "We'll talk about that later, Ruby, get those people moving now."

"All Dragon units, this is Dragon Control," Mom radioed. "We have a Code Twenty situation at three, six, eight—two, five, eight. Report to that location and await further orders. How copy?"

All three Griffins answered instantly as they wheeled around in the sky and headed for the search team on the ground. Gunner and Leg's Dragon One Four was the first to reach their location. On the way, Zoomie had been in contact with them and with Buzz, working out a new plan, and was ready to go into operation. Before the chopper had even skidded to a halt he had the side door open and the snowmobile rigged for instant deployment.

As soon as the snowmobile and his search team was on the ground, Gunner took his ship back up into the air to make way for the next Griffin to land.

When all of his men had been assembled, Zoomie gave them a short briefing. "We've just had a distress call from Mojo, but we can't make contact with him again. Buzz thinks they were calling from a chopper and that the

179

chopper has gone down somewhere around here. Keep it well spread out and look for any signs of it or our two guys. Keep in contact and report everything you see."

The platoon leader looked at the hopeful faces of his men. "Any questions?"

"Okay then, let's move it out."

The four snowmobiles deployed well out to the flanks as the rest of the men spread out and started up the side of the mountain. Overhead, the three Griffins split up to cover as much ground as they could with their sensors.

This time, Wolff and Mojo had their arms handcuffed tightly behind their backs before they were loaded onto the rear of the snowmobiles and driven back up the side of the mountain. Once they were safely inside the facility, they were hustled into the control room to face Buck Sloan.

The politician was not happy to see the two cops. "You boys just fucked up in a major way," he said quietly. "And I can't have that."

"And just how's that?" Wolff asked. He knew the answer to that question himself, but he could not help needling the anonymous leader of this mysterious operation.

"As far as I'm concerned, you're the one who's fucked up, mister. You're the one who's holding Federal officers captive. And speaking of that, just who in the hell do you think you are, and what in the hell's going on here?"

Sloan looked at them for a long moment. The urge to kick the living shit out of that smart-mouthed cop was overwhelming, but he smiled instead. "That's not important for you to know right now. What *is* important is that if you and your buddy get out of line again, I'm going to have you shot right here and now. I can't afford to have any more problems with you two."

Just then one of the technicians shouted for Sloan to come to his console. "I'm picking up movement right below the mountain," he said.

"Let me see."

Sloan worked the controls of the remote optical pickups and focused in on one of the Tac Platoon snowmobiles making its way through the woods in the valley below the mountain. The telelens on the pickup plainly showed the yellow letters TPF on the front cowling of the dark blue machine. There was no mistaking who it was.

The breath caught in Sloan's throat. It was the Tac Force and they were looking for the two men he held captive. They must have spotted that damned chopper.

"Damn!"

"How long till the satellite is in position?" he asked the man beside him.

"It won't be over the horizon for another fifty-five minutes."

"Shit!" Sloan muttered. "Alert Bowman and tell him to get his men into position to take those guys out if they get too close."

"Yes, sir."

The politician turned back abruptly to face Wolff and Mugabe's guards. "Put these two assholes back in their cell," he snapped. "And you'd better make sure that they fucking stay there this time."

"Yes, sir."

"You heard the man," one of the guards snarled as he slammed the muzzle of his assault rifle into Wolff's side. "Move it!"

The other guard motioned with his pistol and the two cops started walking. For the first time since their crash, they knew that Dragon Flight hadn't forgotten them. Zoomie and the boys were out there looking for them, but there was no way that the Tac cops could discover anything about the facility buried under the mountain unless Wolff and Mugabe could somehow free themselves and warn Zoomie that they were walking into an ambush.

Gunner and Legs were on their second pass over the base of the mountain when Sandra's sensor monitor lit up like a Christmas tree. "I've got something," she said, keeping her voice calm. "The mass proximeter and IR are showing a big mass of metal that's warmer than its surroundings. It might be a chopper on the ground."

"Give it to me."

Punching the keys on her console, Sandra instantly sent the sensor data to Gunner's navigation computer and switched over to her optical sighting system as Gunner banked the Griffin over on a new heading.

"There it is," she said excitedly, pointing through the Griffin's canopy. "Left front, right at the edge of that stand of trees."

"I've got it," Gunner said, keying his throat mike. "Tac One," he radioed, "this is One Four. We have spotted a downed chopper at three, seven, two—two, five, zero. Meet us at that location."

"This is Tac One," Zoomie radioed back. "I copy three, seven, two—two, five, zero. I'll be there in one zero." As Gunner flared out for a landing next to the crashed Bell, Sandra saw that the location beacons for all four snowmobiles were converging on the site at top speed. Maybe the New Year had brought them good luck after all.

When Wolff and Mugabe turned the corner into the hallway leading back to their cell, the pilot stumbled and fell face first against the wall. Alarmed, Mojo moved to help him and was shoved back.

"Hey, asshole!" the guard with the rifle said, slamming the muzzle of the weapon into the pilot's ribs. "Watch where you're going!"

Wolff tried to bring his cuffed hands around to balance himself against the wall. "I hit my head in the crash," he muttered. "I think I'm going to pass out."

"Tough shit," the guard said, nudging him with the muzzle of his rifle again. "I don't give a fuck if you're dying. Move it!"

Wolff caught Mojo's eye and a look passed between them. If they were ever going to get out of this, it had to be before they were locked in their cell again.

Pushing himself off the wall, Wolff kicked backward with his right leg. His boot heel caught his guard between the legs, crushing his testicles. The man's breath went out with a whoosh and the rifle dropped from his hands as he fell to the floor doubled up with pain.

Mugabe's guard spun around, trying to bring his pistol to bear on Wolff, but he was standing too close. Mugabe rammed his elbows into the man's ribs, knocking him off balance.

Wolff spun around to face him and lashed out again, his high kick catching Mugabe's man in the solar plexus. When the guard doubled over, Mugabe threw himself against him, slamming his head against the wall with skull-splitting force. As the second guard crumpled to the ground, Wolff sensed movement behind him. Spinning around, he saw the man he had kicked reaching for his fallen rifle.

Wolff kicked out again and caught the man in the throat with the toe of his flight boot. The guard gurgled and turned red in the face. He clawed at his throat and his eyes bulged as he tried to force air through a crushed larynx. He was dead in sixty seconds.

Mugabe dispatched his man with a kick to the temple

and the hall was silent again.

"Quick," Wolff whispered, dropping down to his knees. "Get the rifle."

Mugabe spun around and, kneeling down, grabbed the rifle with his cuffed hands. He found the trigger and flicked the weapon off safety. Wolff knelt beside him and, holding his cuffed hands as far away from his body as he could, maneuvered the muzzle of the rifle until it was pressed against the middle link of the handcuffs. He turned his head to the side and closed his eyes. "Fire!"

Mojo triggered the assault rifle and the bullet smashed through the link, freeing the pilot's hands. Wolff brought his arms around in front of him and rubbed his stinging wrists. He was still wearing the cuffs themselves, but he could live with that for now. He snatched the rifle from Mojo's hands and glanced up and down the hall, but no one had responded to the rifle shot.

"Okay," he said. "Hold your arms out." The second shot freed Mugabe's hands. The gunner grimaced as he used his right hand to pull his left arm back in front of him.

"How's the arm?" Wolff asked.

"I can shoot this one-handed," Mojo said as he scooped up the pistol his guard had dropped. "Let's get the fuck outta here."

Wolff grabbed the assault rifle and checked the load in the magazine. He stripped the ammo pouches from his guard and looked down the hall as he strapped them around his waist. "Let's try for the back door again," he said.

Mojo pulled the spare magazine out of the guard's belt pouch and stuffed it in his pocket. "We can go through the basement as far as I care. Let's just get outta here!"

Just then they both heard the sound of men running down the hall. "Quick," Wolff hissed, pulling Mojo along with him. "Back this way."

Their escape route cut off, the two men turned and ran deeper into the facility. They had to find some place to get under cover fast.

Chapter Twenty-three

Medicine Mountain; 1 January

The first thing that Zoomie noticed when he arrived at the crashed chopper were the boot prints sunk deeply into the snow around the machines and the tracks of the snowmobiles. Someone had definitely been here before them, but who had they been and where had they gone?

He quickly checked out the cockpit of the Bell and found it empty of anything that might have told him who had been flying it. He did find that the VHF radio was switched over to the Guard channel. Mom had been right, the radio message she had picked up had come from this machine.

It wasn't much to go on, but it was enough to convince Zoomie that Wolff and Mugabe had not simply been lost in the woods for this past week. They had been held captive somewhere and had managed to escape before being forced down again. The question was, where were they being held? The only structures for miles around were the deserted cabin and that survivalist's compound.

Wherever they were, though, Zoomie now had fresh tracks to follow.

As soon as all of his men and the snowmobiles had been assembled, Zoomie checked them over to see what he had to work with. The Tac Platoon hadn't expected to go into a combat operation today and they weren't wearing their full tactical gear. At least half of his men, however, were wearing their flack vests under their parkas because of the cold, and by borrowing equipment and ammunition from their buddies, they were able to come up with full basic loads.

Half a platoon was better than nothing, and after reporting back to Buzz, Zoomie loaded his two Tac teams onto the backs of the snowmobiles and moved out. Driving the lead snowmobile, Zoomie followed the tracks in the snow. There had been at least two machines following in each other's tracks, maybe more, and as far as he could see, they had gone right up to the base of the mountain. He didn't have any idea why they had gone up there, but he'd find out soon enough.

As Bowman's mountain men scrambled to get to their defensive positions around the mountain hideout, Sloan watched Zoomie's men make their way up to the south side of the mountain. His monitors showed some dozen armed men approaching the rocks at the base of the rock face on snowmobiles. Another dozen or so cops had remained behind at the chopper, but those on the snowmobiles were more than enough to cause him a great deal of trouble if they discovered the entrance to the facility.

Sloan's monitors didn't show the tracks made by the snowmobiles that had picked Wolff and Mugabe up at the crashed chopper, and he didn't know that Zoomie was following them. He still thought that there was a chance the cops would not discover the mine shaft, so he did not order Bowman to stop them yet. He was hoping against hope that he could complete New Dawn without having to get into a firefight with the Tac Force.

Zoomie saw that the snowmobile tracks he had been

following disappeared into a maze of boulders some two hundred meters from the base of the mountain. He brought his machine to a halt and checked out the ground in front of him with his field glasses. On the other side of the rocks there was a dark spot at the base of the rugged cliffs. It looked like there might be some kind of opening in the mountain, a mine shaft, perhaps.

Whatever it was, it was a perfect place for an ambush. It was time to dismount and go it the rest of the way on foot. He radioed his intentions back to Sergeant Garcia and the men he had left with the crashed chopper before leaving the snowmobiles. Then he quickly grouped his men into a tactical formation and started through the rocks.

Bowman's men had been given orders to hold their fire until they heard from the control center, but these men were not trained troops. They were little more than a mob of criminals, malcontents, and social misfits who had come together for the good money Sloan paid. Several of them were good fighting men, but discipline and following orders had never been their strong suits. And they were bored from weeks of inactivity inside the mountain.

One of the mountain men saw the distant figure of a Tac cop fill the sight of his rifle and couldn't resist. Taking a deep breath, he flicked the selector switch on his 7.62mm FN FAL assault rifle down to semiauto fire and slowly squeezed the trigger. The shot echoed from the rocks and the cop pitched over backward.

For a moment there was silence on the mountainside as the report of the shot echoed away. Then all hell broke loose. Thinking that the order to open fire had been given, Bowman's mountain men all opened up at once. Even if they didn't have a target lined up in their sights, they fired anyway.

The Tac cops dove for cover in the rocks and snow-drifts. A hail of automatic weapons fire came from the base of the cliffs, splattering snow in Zoomie's face. He dove for cover behind the nearest rock and frantically tried to find a way out of their exposed position.

They sure as hell weren't going to make it up to the mine shaft the way they were going. He looked to both sides, trying to find another approach, but whoever had set this thing up had sure as hell known what he was doing. There *were* no covered approaches. Period. If they were going to get up there, they were going to have to do it out in the open right in the face of those guns.

Zoomie didn't mind laying his life on the line; he did it all the time. But usually when he did it he knew what he was doing it for and he had backup firepower from the Griffins to help even up the odds. This time, he had no idea what he was facing, and while the choppers refueled he and his people were totally on their own. All they could do was to keep their heads down until he could get the Griffins back on station to lay a little suppressive fire on those gun positions.

He switched over to the command frequency and keyed his mike. "Dragon Control, this is Tac One."

"Control, go."

"This is Tac One, advise Command One that we are under fire from an unknown force at the base of the south face of Medicine Mountain. We have taken cover in a rockpile, but they've got us pinned down and we're unable to maneuver against these people. Urgently request Griffin support soonest. How copy?"

"This is Command One," Buzz's voice broke in over the earphones of Zoomie's helmet. "What's the size of your opposition?"

"I'd say there's at least a dozen of them and they're all armed with automatic weapons. So far I haven't seen any big stuff, it's all assault rifle fire."

"Just hang tight," Buzz said. "I'll get the Griffins back to you ASAP."

"Tac One, copy. Tell 'em to turn up the wick."

Sloan was furious as he watched the firefight start on the monitors. God damn that Bowman! Now there was no way to keep the Tac Force from discovering the entrance to the mountain facility. Even if Bowman was able to beat off this attack, Sloan know that more troops would come, maybe even the army would get into the act. He could deal with the chopper cops, but not the army.

If Bowman didn't get himself killed today Sloan was going to do the honors himself. All this work down the drain because that fucking redneck couldn't follow orders.

The politician turned back to the satellite control station. Before he took care of Bowman, however, there was still the matter of the Diablo Canyon nuclear plant. Regardless of the outcome of the firefight outside, he had to go through with the New Dawn operation. But he had to make sure that Bowman held the cops off long enough for him to do what had to be done.

Just then he saw one of the Tac cops reach up to key the mike on his helmet radio and he got an idea. He turned to the technician manning the EMP weapon. "Can you aim at those cops?" he asked.

The man checked his target radar. "No sweat."

Sloan smiled. "Put the beam on wide dispersion and hose that whole area down," he ordered.

The weapons technician rolled back the camouflaged door concealing the EMP weapon and brought it up into firing position. It was not designed as an area weapon, but he was able to defocus the beam and, traversing the dish from right to left, cover the south slope of the mountain with electromagnetic pulse radiation.

Sloan was fully aware that not only would the EMP kill the cop's radios, it would also knock out his communications with Bowman and his men. But Sloan didn't care what happened to those people right now, they had always been the expendable part of the New Dawn operation. The more of them that got killed out there, the fewer there would be left to finger him if they were captured.

"That should do it," the EMP weapon man said. "I covered the whole south face."

Sloan glanced up at the monitors. The EMP pulse had even taken out the close-in remote cameras, but it didn't matter. He knew what was going on out there. "Don't power down," he told the man. "Keep an eye out for those choppers. If you see any of them, blast them, too."

"Yes, sir," the man said.

Zoomie was talking to Sergeant Garcia when his helmet radio went completely dead. He shook his head and tapped the side of his helmet, but the tac display on the inside of his face shield didn't reappear and the hiss of the radios over his headphones was gone. He switched back to the command frequency and tried to call Mom, but the radio was dead; he couldn't reach anyone.

"Okay," he muttered. "We'll have to do this the hard way."

Reaching under his flak vest, he pulled out a chrome whistle on a chain, an old fashioned cop's whistle. Raising his face shield, he put the whistle to his lips and blew three sharp, shrill blasts. A few seconds later, answering whistle blasts came from both his right and his left. It had been a long time since the Tac Platoon had practiced ground tactics in a radioless environment, and he just hoped that his men could remember back that far. He also hoped to hell that he could remember the whistle signals for that matter.

Back at the jump CP at the Forest Service airstrip,

Mom had been monitoring the tactical input from Zoomie's command helmet. Suddenly there was a burst of static and the Tactical Platoon monitors blanked out.

Reaching out, she attempted to call up the images again, but they were gone. For some reason Zumwald wasn't transmitting anything.

"Tac One," she keyed her throat mike. "This is Dragon Control, come in please."

A rush of static was all that came in over Zoomie's command frequency.

She switched over to the internal Tac Platoon frequency. "Any Tac Platoon station, any Tac Platoon station, this is Control, come in please."

There was still no answer.

Mom swiveled around in her chair. "Buzz," she said. "I think we've got a problem with Lieutenant Zumwald. His radios have gone out."

"What?"

"Yes, sir, everything's dead. I can't raise any of them. It's like they turned all their radios off."

"How about the locator beacons?"

Medicine Mountain was close enough that they should be able to pick up the personal locator beacon that every man wore as part of his equipment. Mom keyed in the locator response signal. Nothing.

"They're all dead too," she said. "Those things are supposed to last forever. What in the hell is going on up there?"

Buzz was thoughtful for a moment. "Whatever it is, it's the same thing that happened to Wolff and Mugabe. They lost their beacons too. Remember?"

"Oh, God!" Mom said softly. "Red said that the electronics were burned out on their Griffin."

"Whatever's up there, it can obviously take out all of our electronics. We've got to pull the other Griffins back before they crash too."

"But what about Zoomie?"

Buzz's face was grim. "I'm afraid that they're just going to have to go it on their own until we can figure out what we can do to help him. Get on the horn to the Griffins while we still can and tell them to hold off."

"Yes, sir."

Chapter Twenty-four

Medicine Mountain; 1 January

Gunner and Sandra had completed their refueling and were almost back to the battle site when they received Mom's warning to hold off until they could find out why the Tac Platoon's radios had gone off the air.

"What could take out all those radios at the same time like that?" Gunner asked. He was a good pilot, but he left the scientific end of their missions to Legs and her sophisticated array of sensors.

Sandra frowned. "I don't know, but I got a strange spike on my radiation monitor about the time that their radios went out."

"What kind of spike?"

"Some kind of electromagnetic radiation," she said. "It was stronger than anything I've ever seen and it lasted for several seconds."

"Could someone be shooting some kind of radiation weapon at them?"

"That would account for it," she said thoughtfully. "But from where?"

"With these forests all around here," Gunner said, scanning their surroundings. "The only location that would have a good enough field of fire to cover such a large area would have to be someplace high. Someplace like up on that mountain."

Sandra glanced over at the mountain in the distance. "You want to check it out?" she asked.

Gunner grinned. "Why not? All that can happen is that we'll end up getting shot down the same way that Mojo and Wolff bought it."

Gunner brought the Griffin down low, keeping to the edge of the trees along the base of the mountain while Sandra turned her full sensor array on the peak looming over them. The first pass showed nothing and Gunner was about to take his ship in for a closer look when Sandra shouted. "Lock-on! I've got targeting-radar locked on."

"Where's it coming from?"

She looked up from her console. "It's coming from the mountain!"

Gunner threw his ship into a hard bank and headed back for cover in the forest, trying to hide his ship in the natural breaks and clearings in the trees.

"It's still tracking us!" Sandra shouted, frantically stabbing at the ECM controls in a vain attempt to break the lock-on. "I can't jam it!"

"End of the line," Wolff said, peering around the corner of the corridor into the big room in front of them. "It looks like we've run into the control room for what ever this operation is."

Mojo joined him for a quick look and saw a scene out of a science fiction movie. A dozen blue-coated technicians sat behind consoles, computer monitors, and huge television screens. He couldn't spot the leader who had interrogated them before, but he figured that he had to be around somewhere; this was too big an operation to run on its own.

"Sweet bleeding Jesus!" Wolff whispered. "Look at that monitor right in the middle, the big one. Do you know where that is?"

Mojo looked and saw a TV screen displaying some kind

of huge, hi-tech facility. "No."

"It's the Diablo Canyon nuclear power plant right outside San Luis Obispo, California."

"You sure?"

"Yes damn it," Wolff snapped. "I used to date a girl from San Luis. She was a fanatic antinuke freak and was always protesting the fucking place. I'd have to pick her up from the picket lines when I wanted to take her out. I finally quit dating her because all she wanted to talk about was radiation, not sex."

"What in the hell is a nuke plant doing up on that monitor?"

"Beats me," Wolff said. "But look at that long screen right above it, the one with the world map on it. That guy said something about a satellite, and isn't that some kind of satellite tracking screen?"

"Oh, shit," Mojo said. "I think you're right. And, it's showing the path of a military satellite."

"Military?" Wolff frowned. "How do you know that?"

"The orbital path," Mugabe said. "See how the track swings back and forth to cover everything from pole to pole. I think it's showing the orbit of an SDI bird, one of the missile-killer satellites."

Suddenly the path on the tracking screen changed and the base map changed to show an enlarged section of the Southern California coastline and the Pacific Ocean.

"Aren't those SDI birds armed with lasers?" Wolff asked.

"Yeah, why?"

"What would happen if that laser was fired at the plant?"

"I don't know," Mojo frowned. "The lasers are designed to work in space, in a vacuum. Air scatters the beam and diffuses it. But I don't know."

"Even firing through the air, though," Wolff said, "couldn't it melt the dome at that plant. Like they show them doing in the movies?"

"Oh, sweet Jesus," Mojo breathed. "They're trying to

blow up the place."

"What the fuck's going on here?"

"I don't know," Mojo shook his head. "But I just spotted what I think are a set of manual controls for controlling the satellite and maybe even firing the weapons. See that pair of joysticks by that control panel under the satellite monitor, the ones that look like they're the controls for a huge arcade game?"

"Yeah."

"I think they can be used to fly the SDI bird into a new orbit."

"We've got to do something to stop them."

"Just what do you have in mind, Superman?" Mojo said. "You seem to forget that there's over a dozen guys in that room and most of them are packing guns. And at last count, there's only two of us."

"We just can't sit here and watch them blow up that plant," Wolff said. "The fallout will contaminate half of Southern California."

"But it ain't going to help the surfers if we get ourselves killed too."

"Fuck that," Wolff shot back. "I can't just hide here and watch this go down."

Just then an alarm sounded throughout the facility. Someone had stumbled onto the bodies of the guards they had killed.

"Ah, shit," Wolff muttered, looking around for a place to hide.

"Rick!" Mojo hissed. "Look at that monitor over on the far left."

Wolff looked and saw a large TV screen showing a picture of a Griffin chopper. The big white numbers One Four showed plainly on its dark blue nose. It was Gunner and Legs! As he watched, the man sitting in front of the screen punched the keys on his controls and cross hairs appeared on the screen, superimposed on the image of the chopper.

Wolff didn't hesitate for a second. He didn't know exactly what the screen was, but he knew a weapon's sight when he saw one. Snapping the butt of his assault rifle up to his shoulder, he fired off a short burst at the man sitting in front of the screen. He shifted his point of aim and fired again, taking out the monitor as well.

For a short moment there was silence as the shots echoed through the control room, followed by the sound of broken glass crashing to the floor. Then all hell broke loose. Several of the technicians scrambled for their weapons, but most of them jumped up and dashed for the door at the other end of the room. Several well-aimed shots took out the men with guns, and in less than a minute, the two chopper cops had the control room completely to themselves.

Wolff shut the door behind them and slid the locks into place. "Now," he said, "let's see what we have here."

Gunner violently threw his ship all over the sky, trying to break the radar lock-on. Bringing the speeding chopper dangerously close to the ground, he wove a dangerous path through the towering trees, his rotor tip vortexes shaking the branches. In the left-hand seat, Sandra's fingers flew over the ECM controls, frantically sending jamming signals on all frequencies to break the lock-on. "Run for it!" she shouted. "I can't lose them!"

Suddenly the ruby glow of the threat warning light winked out. The tracking radar beam was gone. "It's disappeared," Sandra said, her eyes scanning her readouts. "Whatever it was, it's gone."

Gunner eased off the throttle and brought the Griffin back up above the treetops. "Keep an eye on it," he said. "I'm going to try it again."

"You think you can do anything with this?" Wolff asked

as Mojo slipped into the technician's chair in front of the satellite screen.

Mugabe scanned the unfamiliar controls. "It looks simple enough," he said, resting his fingers on the keyboard. "Kind of like a video game for grownups."

Keeping an eye on the satellite flight path displayed on the screen, he moved one of the joysticks. Nothing seemed to happen, but a few seconds later, the flight path moved a little to the north. "I've got it," he shouted.

He had to remember that because of the distance the radio signal had to travel to reach the satellite, he had to anticipate a short delay before it responded, but he had control of an SDI killer satellite. Now what in the hell was he going to do with the damned thing? First, he would see what he could do to turn the laser off or put it back on "Safe."

Mojo studied the controls under the panel marked "Targeting." "Shit!" he muttered. "This fucking thing's Greek to me."

"Doesn't it have a menu that tells you what to do?" Wolff asked.

Mugabe typed the word *Menu* and hit the enter key. Nothing happened. "I knew it couldn't be that simple," he growled.

"Try *Sequence*," Wolff suggested, leaning over his shoulder to watch the screen.

Mojo typed the word *Sequence* and the monitor came alive. "Bingo!"

He studied the menu for a moment and started typing, his fingers flying over the keyboard. Sub-menus appeared with a list of commands as he worked his way through the weapons firing commands. Suddenly he stopped cold. "Rick," he said softly, "this thing's on some kind of automatic firing sequence."

"What!"

"It's set to fire the laser in three minutes, and I can't turn it off. It takes some kind of fail-safe code to do that, and I don't know the code."

Suddenly Mojo had a thought. If these guys were planning to blow up a nuclear power plant with the laser, maybe it could be used to put this facility out of action as well. If he couldn't turn it off, he could at least try to aim the weapon someplace else. He got back on the keyboard and discovered that all he had to do was to call up the targeting map and reorient the satellite with the joysticks.

Wolff kept silent as Mojo searched through the menus to find out how to change the targeting maps. Finally the monitor switched from the Southern California map to one showing the western United States. By calling up magnification, he soon had a map of northern Colorado and southern Wyoming on the screen, with a red pip blinking over the representation of Medicine Mountain on the map. "Got it!" he muttered.

Mugabe punched in further magnification and the screen changed to show an enlarged map of an area only two kilometers across. Medicine Mountain and its approaches took up almost all of the screen.

"That tunnel they took us into is on the south side of this thing, right?"

"Yeah, why?"

"I'm trying to figure out where in the hell to aim that thing to take this place out. I can't just blow up the whole damned mountain, it's a national park."

Wolff choked off a laugh. "Anything is better than letting it hit Diablo Canyon," he said. "I don't think the president will mind losing a mountain if we can keep from blasting a nuke plant."

Mojo moved the red pip over to the south side of the mountain and stopped it.

"Here it goes," he said, looking up from the keyboard.

"We're about to become the first live fire target for an SDI satellite. Wolff's eyes watched the digital counter tick off the remaining few minutes. "Let's get the hell outta here before that thing goes off. I really don't feel like being the world's first laser-barbecued cop."

Chapter Twenty-five

Medicine Mountain; 1 January

Just moments before Wolff and Mugabe had arrived at the control room, Buck Sloan had left to go to his security office. Since the satellite had been given its targeting instructions and the automatic firing sequence had been initiated, there had been nothing more for him to do in the control room, so instead of waiting for the clock to tick off, he had gone to see what he could do to affect the outcome of the battle between Bowman's men and the Tac Force. Even with the panic that would follow New Dawn, he didn't need to have cops poking around inside his facility.

He was trying to contact Bowman when the first of the laser bolts streaked down from deep space to hit Medicine Mountain. The shaft of blinding blue light touched down on the south face of the mountain right above the EMP weapon's hiding place. When the beam touched down, snow and ice flashed into superheated steam and rocks exploded. The devastation touched off an avalanche that went cascading down the side of the mountain.

Part of the rock fall sealed off the EMP weapon's aperture and crushed the device to scrap metal. More of the falling rocks slammed into the side of a bank of solar energy collectors, cutting off the power feed lines into the facility. More of them rained down on Bowman and his men. Alarms went off inside the facility as the laser bored deeper and deeper into the mountain.

Sloan didn't even try to find out what had happened. At the first sound of an explosion he spun around and raced for the upper corridor leading to the underground chopper hanger. As he ran, he heard more explosions as the killer satellite's laser continued to tear into his mountain facility. It was all over—SOLCO, his campaign for the nation's highest office, everything. All he could do now was to make a run for it and hope that he could stay ahead of the cops.

Gunner and Legs were approaching Zoomie's positions when the laser started firing. In the glare of the bright mountain sun, the beam itself couldn't be seen, but the damage it was causing could. As they watched, they saw the side of the mountain explode like a bomb had been dropped on it. Huge boulders flew up into the air and shattered on impact like giant grenades. Entire snow fields shaken loose by the violence started slipping down the mountain.

They also saw Bowman's white-uniformed men running from the base of the mountain toward the Tac Platoon. They were firing their weapons as they ran.

Gunner knew that he couldn't talk to Zoomie, but it was obvious that they could use a little help. "Control," he radioed. "This is One Four. We're going in to give Tac One a hand."

"Control, copy," Mom radioed back. "Keep me informed."

Gunner nosed his ship over and headed down to lend him a hand with a little fire support. He'd worry about what was tearing up the mountain as soon as he took care of Zoomie's little problem.

Sloan ran through the door that opened out into the excavated cavern that served as his hanger and dogged it shut behind him. Parked against the back wall of the cavern was his way out of this mess. The SDI satellite codes weren't all that Sloan's money had bought; it had also netted him a black market, ex-U.S. Army AH-64X Super Apache attack helicopter.

The gunship was part of a shipment that had been bound for the Israeli defense forces when it was hijacked by South African mercenaries. The stolen Apache had been expensive, but Sloan had not been able to resist a deal like that at any price. Along with being an engineer, he was also an experienced pilot, and every pilot dreams of owning his own fighter. Even a rotary-winged fighter.

This particular machine was a cross between the standard Army Super Apache attack chopper and the proposed Navy Sea Apache version that had been canceled in the great military budget cuts of the post-Cold War era. The Israelis, however, had wanted the air-to-air fighting capabilities of the Sea Apache as well as the tank-busting armament of the Army versions, so the X models they had ordered incorporated both weapons systems. When Sloan bought his gunship, the South Africans had thrown in a pair of AIM-9P Sidewinder air-to-air missiles to sweeten the deal. These missiles were now mounted on the stub wing launchers of the Super Apache.

The TPF Griffins were generally considered to be the most sophisticated chopper gunship in the air. But that was only if the Super Apache was not being considered for those honors. This bastardized chopper edged out the TPF Griffins because it didn't have to give any up space or weight penalty to noncombat considerations. Sloan's Super Apache was a one hundred percent fighting machine. It was just as fast and even better armed and armored as the Tac Force Griffins, and it was the only thing that really stood a chance in air-to-air combat with them.

As a pilot, Sloan had enjoyed playing with the potent gunship, but now that everything had gone tits up, it was time to stop playing around with it. The Super Apache was his ticket out of here. In just a couple hours flight time, he would be south of the border, and nothing short of Air Force fighters could stop him.

Sloan always kept his ship topped off in a flight-ready status, and it only took seconds for him to whip the covers off the cannon barrel and the missile warheads before strapping himself into the pilot's seat and firing up the twin GE turbines. As soon as the main rotor came up to speed, he punched in the code to open the camouflaged hanger doors in the side of the mountain.

Rising to a low hover, Sloan nudged forward on the cyclic stick and nosed the Apache out past the open doors to the rock ledge outside. A twist of the throttle brought the rotors up to speed, and he hauled up on the collective control. The Apache leaped into the air, banking away to clear the side of the mountain.

As soon as he was in the clear, Sloan hit the overrev switch on the instrument panel and the turbines screamed as the ship rapidly gained airspeed. Before he made his escape, he was going to insure that he was not followed and that no one reported where he was going. He was going to blast those damned Tac Force choppers out of the sky.

The first TPF Griffin he spotted bore the big white numbers One Four on the nose. The ship was making a firing run against the remnants of Bowman's security force dug in on the mountainside. Sloan banked the Apache over to take up a firing position behind it. He reached out to arm the missiles, but then stopped and activated the nose turret instead. This was an easy shot for the 25mm chain gun, and he might need the Sidewinders later if anyone tried to get in his way as he headed south.

In the cockpit of Dragon One Four, Gunner and Legs were concentrating on the air support gun runs they were making for Zoomie's troops as the Tac Platoon mopped up the last remnants of Sloan's mountain men. With the Tac Platoon's radios knocked out, the flyers were going about their work very carefully, checking twice before they fired on any target. The battle was almost over, and this was no time to screw up and bag a couple of Zoomie's men by mistake.

They were so engrossed in spotting their targets that they didn't see the fleeting shadow of Sloan's diving Apache flash past them as he hauled his gunship into a firing position high above and to the rear of the Griffin.

The first indication that they had an enemy in the sky behind them was when a burst of tracer fire from the Apache's 25mm chain gun sparkled past their canopy.

Gunner reacted by instinct and that was the only thing that saved their lives. Stomping down on the rudder pedal and slamming the cyclic all the way over against the right stop, he let the torque of the main rotor snap the Griffin's tail around to the left as he pulled the nose into a hard right-hand turn.

Sloan's second burst of fire missed the main cabin and slammed into the rear compartment of the Griffin. Like the rest of the ship, the rear compartment was armored against light-caliber fire, but it was not armored against something as powerful as the Apache's chain gun.

Sloan's 25mm HE shells smashed through the Lexan side windows and exploded inside the compartment. The Kevlar seats saved Gunner and Legs from the red-hot shell fragments, but they tore through the inside of the ship, shredding the air frame and smashing the flight controls. The Griffin staggered in the air as the shells hammered into her. Hydraulic oil squirted from the severed lines and was ignited by the hot shell fragments. In seconds, the inside of the ship was a blazing inferno.

Sloan smiled as he watched his cannon shells slam into Gunner's Griffin. His smile grew when greasy black smoke started pouring out of the stricken chopper's fuselage as it started down toward the snow-covered mountain below. He pressed the chain gun's trigger again and saw more hits sparkle against the armor plating. Pieces of the skin ripped loose and flew off in the slipstream as the chopper went into a steeper dive.

Inside the Griffin, Gunner fought to keep the crippled ship in the air, going into the hydraulic backup system to try to save control of the tail rotor. "I'm losing it!" he yelled over to Sandra as the ship started going into a spin. "Get on the controls with me!"

Sandra's feet slammed down to the rudder pedals and her hands flew to the duplicate copilot's cyclic and collective controls. Following Gunner's movements, she added her weight to the stiff control sticks. Slowly the Griffin stopped turning around it's main axis and leveled out. "We've got to put it down!" Gunner yelled.

"Hurry!" Sandra yelled back as she watched the exhaust temperature gage run up into the end of the red zone. "The turbines are overheating!"

Gunner aimed the plummeting ship at an open patch of snow. "Hang on!"

After racing through dark corridors, Wolff and Mugabe finally reached the door they had escaped from before and broke out into the open. In the panic inside the facility, no one had bothered to stop them or ask them who they were. It was every man for himself.

They raced out into the clearing right on the heels of two of Sloan's men. Neither of them were armed, and when they took cover from the falling rocks, Wolff and Mojo had no trouble taking them into custody. The two men were so stunned that they didn't even try to resist.

After taking their guns from them, Wolff looked up just in time to see Sloan's gunship dive down on the unsuspecting Dragon One Four, its nose turret spitting flame. He saw

One Four take hits and start to spin down out of control, smoke pouring from the shattered windows of the rear compartment.

"Fuck!" Wolff howled as the Super Apache flew in closer to pour even more fire into the helpless Griffin. Legs and Gunner were being murdered in the air and there was nothing he could do to stop it.

The pilot frantically looked around the sky and spotted another Griffin keeping low to the tops of the trees as it chased men on the ground. As it banked off to the side Wolff saw the white numbers One Two on her nose. He remembered that one of his prisoners had a radio on his belt. "Gimme that radio!" he yelled, snatching it from his belt.

Mojo followed his glance and knew what Wolff had in mind. A little payback was in order here.

Wolff didn't know what frequency the radio was set on, but the Griffin should be monitoring all bands and should pick up his transmission. "Dragon One Two," he radioed. "This is Dragon Lead, Come in."

"Wolfman!" Browning, the pilot of One Two shouted. "You're alive! Where the hell are you?"

"Mojo and I are standing in an open clearing halfway up the north face of the mountain." Wolff replied. "Get your ass down here and get us outta here. Now!"

"Good copy," Browning answered. "I'm on the way. Hang on."

"Just get your ass down here."

Sloan pulled away from the stricken Griffin and climbed back up into the sky. That should take care of that one; now where in the hell was that other TPF machine?

He glanced around and saw that the other TPF Griffin was heading in for a landing at the small clearing on the side of the mountain. He didn't know what it was doing down there, but it couldn't cause him any trouble now. By the time it could get back in the air, he would be miles away. He banked his Apache over on her side and pushed the nose down to pick up speed.

He watched as the needle on his airspeed indicator flashed past the numbers and the turbine RPM needle hovered at the far end of the red line. The Apache was flying as fast as it could possibly go. In a few more minutes he would be completely safe from any possible pursuit.

Chapter Twenty-six

High over Medicine Mountain; 1 January

Browning brought his machine in for a hot landing, brushing the skids against the snow as he hauled full back on the cyclic to kill his forward speed. No sooner had the chopper skidded to a stop than Wolff ran up to the pilot's door and jerked it open.

"Get out," he shouted, pulling at Browning's arm.

Browning looked down at him like he was out of his mind. With a week and half's worth of beard, wild hair, and filthy flight suit, Wolff looked like he had just come off a week-long drunk. "But, Rick . . ." the pilot started to protest.

"I don't have time to argue with you," Wolff grabbed at the buckle of his shoulder harness. "Get your ass out of there and give me your helmet! Now! You, too!" he shouted over at the gunner.

The pilot quickly unbuckled and was stepping down when Wolff pushed past him and slid into the pilot's seat. "And keep track of those two," Wolff pointed at his prisoners as he snatched the helmet out of Browning's hand and jammed it on his head.

Mugabe was right behind him, but he was still fumbling one-handed with his shoulder harness when Wolff hauled up on the collective and sent the Griffin screaming up into the sky, her turbines set on maximum overrev.

"Where is that fucker?" Wolff yelled over the intercom.

In the left-hand seat, Mojo rested his left-hand in his lap as he reached out and flicked on his targeting radar and optical sights with his right hand. As soon as they came up, he wrapped the fingers of his good hand around the turret firing controls. He might be hurt, but he was still able to play the game.

"I've got him at a bearing of two twenty heading away from here," he said, reading off his targeting radar. "He's going balls-out and staying down low."

Wolff sent his borrowed machine up in a steep climb. In aerial combat, altitude equals advantage, and he wasn't about to give that bastard an even break. He was out for blood.

Just then, Buzz's voice broke in on the helmet headphones. "Dragon One Two, this is Command One. What's the situation on Wolff and Mugabe?"

Wolff keyed his throat mike. "This is the Wolfman on board Dragon One Two. Be advised that Mojo and I are in hot pursuit of the bandit that shot Gunner and Legs down."

"You're not supposed to be flying!" Buzz radioed back. "Let One Three take care of him."

"Stuff it, Buzz," Wolff shot back, his hand reaching for the radio switch. "I'll get back to you after I splash this bastard." He flicked the command radio off.

"We just had a massive radio failure," he told Mugabe. "Make sure that we report the malfunction to Red when we get back."

Mojo grinned. It was good to be back up in the air with the Wolfman again.

Sloan was far enough away from the mountain that he thought he could switch off the turbine overrev. No one could catch up with him now, and there was no sense in junking his engines when he needed them to take him all

211

the way into the Yucatan Peninsula. He had a small estate in the middle of the jungle and he'd be safe there. The local authorities were all in his pocket and would make sure that he wasn't bothered.

"Yo! Maggot!" he heard a voice over his helmet headphones. He glanced down at the radio frequency readout and saw that the voice was coming in over Guard channel, the international emergency frequency.

"Yes, you, dickhead!" the voice said. "Look behind you!"

Sloan swiveled his head around and saw a dark speck in the sky behind him coming on fast. He slammed the cyclic stick over to rack the Super Apache around in a sharp turn to get a better look.

"Good!" the voice said. "You see me. Now listen real carefully, asshole. You have five seconds to cut your airspeed and turn that ship around before I blow your worthless ass out of the sky."

Sloan frantically switched his radio over to Guard channel. "Who are you?" he asked.

"I'm the Wolfman," the voice said with a laugh. "And I'm your worst fucking nightmare come true. Shut it down now and save yourself a lot of grief."

Now Sloan recognized the voice, it was that smart-mouthed white chopper cop. Somehow he had survived the destruction of the facility and had found himself a helicopter. And if *he* had made it out, it was more than likely that his buddy the black cop was alive too. God damn! He should have just gone ahead and wasted those two while he'd had the chance, instead of trying to keep things neat and tidy.

But no problem, he'd take care of that oversight right now. Never let it be said that Buck Sloan couldn't learn from his mistakes.

Sloan reached out and flicked the governor control back to overrev. Whoever this hotshot cop thought he was, he didn't know who he was fucking around with. Buck Sloan wasn't some stupid asshole trying to fly a load of drugs in under the radar, and he wasn't flying an unarmed chopper, either. He was flying one of the world's hottest attack helicopters and he damned well knew how to use it.

He set the collective pitch control to take advantage of the increased turbine RPM. He was still going to make his escape to southern Mexico, but he wasn't in such a hurry that he couldn't take a few minutes to teach those TPF cops a short but fatal lesson in air-to-air helicopter combat. He reached out and armed the Sidewinder missiles.

Mojo grinned when he saw the Apache wheel around in the sky and turn to face them. "He fell for it," he said. "Now his ass is ours."

"All we've got to do is shoot him down," Wolff replied. "You up to it?"

Mojo flexed his left arm. "I'll have to do it one-handed," he replied. "But I don't see a problem."

"That's good," Wolff said. "Because it looks like that guy's flying a Super Apache, and that thing's real bad news. He's got the same guns we do and even more armor plating, so you're going to have to get in his shorts real fast before he can get in ours."

"Let's do it."

Just then Mojo's threat warning buzzer sounded. "He's got air-to-air missiles!" he shouted as he hit the switches to the ECM module.

Wolff threw the Griffin into a violent evasive maneuver, putting the nose of his ship face on to the bandit. "What kind of missiles?"

Mojo scanned his sensor readouts, "I'm not getting a laser designator or a radar guidance lock-on, so they've got to be heat-seekers."

"Get on the flares!"

The Griffin could be fitted with Black Hole infrared suppressor kits to cut down on the turbine exhaust heat emissions to counter this type of missile. But since Dragon Flight had come north on a search and rescue mission and wasn't expecting to go into combat, those IR kits were sitting in the hanger back in Denver. Without them, Wolff's twin turbines were leaving a heat trail through the cold mountain air that could almost be seen with the naked eye. The infrared-seeking missiles would have no problem finding it and locking on to them.

The only weakness of heat-seeking missiles, however, were that they were fickle. They sought heat sources, the hotter the better. This was why the Griffins were fitted with decoy flares as a defense against them. The flares burned at ten thousand degrees, ten times as hot as the turbine exhausts, and easily lured the missiles away. They had come up against these missiles before and the decoy flares had always worked for them.

"Rick!" Mojo looked frightened. "We don't have any flares."

"Oh, fuck!"

Wolff frantically looked for the sun's position in the sky. It was behind him, high over his right shoulder. He quickly banked the Griffin around so her nose was pointed in the direction of the sun.

The only other defense against heat-seekers was the sun. Even though the sun was millions of miles away, its heat energy reaching the earth was still hotter than anything short of a nuclear explosion. If he could turn his nose into the sun as soon as the missile was launched, putting his ship in a direct line between the missile and the sun, the heat-seeking warhead should lock onto the sun instead of his turbine exhausts. Then at the last possible moment he could dive away and the missile should stay locked onto the sun until it ran out of fuel and fell harmlessly from the sky.

At least that was the way it had always worked in the stories he had read about aerial missile combat over the Middle East and in Vietnam. He had not tried it before himself, but there was always a first time for everything. If it didn't work, there would never be time for anything else.

Sloan smiled when he saw the Griffin turn away from him. Fucking cowards . . . Obviously they had gotten close enough to recognize what they were up against. Well, it wouldn't do them any good to run now. He lined the Griffin up in his gunsight, got a launch tone from the missile warhead, and fired one of the Sidewinders. *Adios*, cop, as they said.

Mugabe caught the missile's launch flare on his sensors. "Launch! Launch!"

Wolff hauled back sharply on his cyclic, pulling the nose of the ship up into a steep climb. Even with his face shield on full antiglare, he still had to squint to aim for the center of the bright ball in the sky.

"It's still tracking us!"

"Tell me when to evade!"

Mojo watched his radar. "Now!"

Wolff chopped his throttle and racked the Griffin over into a sideslip. The missile flashed past them, its warhead locked onto the sun.

"Where is he?" Wolff shouted bringing his ship back upright.

"He's right behind us."

"Hang on and get ready to shoot!"

Since Wolff already had the Griffin in a sharp climb, the fastest way for him to get his ship back into a firing position was to use the oldest maneuver in the history of air fighting, an Immelmann turn. Named after the World War I German ace who had invented it, this maneuver involved a snap roll while in an inside loop, followed by pushing the nose down to send the plane heading back down the way it had come. It was a simple maneuver and had gained its inventor dozens of victories. Even though it had fallen out of favor in the era of missile aerial combat, the Immelmann turn was perfect for what Wolff had in mind—a head-on gun attack.

Sucking the cyclic back into his belly, Wolff sent the Griffin up into a near vertical climb. As soon as the nose was straight up, he slammed the cyclic over against the right stop. The chopper rolled around her long axis until the rotor was where her belly had been only moments before. Hanging on the edge of a stall, Wolff shoved forward on the cyclic, dropping the nose and sending them back down. Suddenly Sloan's Super Apache was right in front of them.

Mojo centered the image of the gunship in the cross hairs of his face shield gunsight and pulled all the way back on the trigger of his chain gun. The airframe shook as the 25mm roared at its maximum rate of fire.

Wolff's maneuver had caught Sloan by surprise, but he reacted well. Right as Mugabe started firing he dumped his collective, destroying his lift, causing the gunship to drop like a stone. Mojo's stream of fire went right over the top of his canopy.

Wolff caught the Super Apache's maneuver and knew that as soon as he flashed over the top of Sloan's gunship, Sloan would zoom up into in a firing position behind him again. And the bastard still had one missile left . . .

Wolff knew that he wouldn't be able to use the sun trick again. He had to do something to neutralize the missile threat. He caught a glimpse of the south side of the mountain and saw that several fires were raging out of control in the ruined facility. The fires might not be as hot as the sun, but they were sure as hell hotter than his turbine exhausts.

Stomping down on his rudder pedals, he snapped the tail of his ship around, lined up on the mountain and twisted his throttle all the way against the stop.

Just as Wolff had predicted, Sloan banked around and got on his tail. Twisting his throttle all the way up against the stop, he raced after the Griffin. In seconds, he was in position to fire his last missile.

"Lock-on!" Mojo yelled.

Wolff aimed the nose of his ship at the biggest fire he could see right as Mojo yelled. "Launch! Launch!

The pilot unconsciously hunched behind his Kevlar seat as he waited for the impact. The armored seat wouldn't do him any good if they got a missile up the tail pipe, but it made him feel better as he dove for the center of the fire.

"Its tracking," Mojo called out. "Get ready. *Now!*"

Wolff stomped down on the right rudder pedal, slammed the cyclic over against the right stop, and pulled maximum pitch to the rotor blades. The speeding Griffin suddenly made a ninety-degree turn in the sky, skidding sideways as Wolff desperately tried to evade the missile. The speeding Sidewinder flashed past the chopper's tail boom and exploded in the middle of the fire.

Now that the missile was gone, it was time to zero this asshole. This shit had gone on long enough. Snapping his machine into a hard, banking turn, Wolff lined up in a good firing position. "Get 'em, Mojo!"

Chapter Twenty-seven

High over Medicine Mountain; 1 January

Mugabe's fingers were on the firing controls as Sloan's Super Apache flashed across their front. His burst of fire went wide as Sloan threw his machine into violent evasive maneuvers. "Rick!" he shouted. "Stay on him!"

Mojo had missed him that time, but the shoe was on the other foot now. With Sloan's missiles gone, there was no way that Wolff was going to let this asshole get away. He owed him one, and it was time for a little payback. Twisting his throttle up against the stop, Wolff racked his ship around to follow the Super Apache.

Sloan proved not to be an easy target, however. He knew how to fly his bird, and with the gunship's turret slaved to fire from the pilot's seat, he was dangerous. Every time Wolff got close enough for Mojo to reach him with the 25mm, he was also within range of the Super Apache's chain gun as well. With the Super Apache's greater armor plating, a head-to-head shootout would only result in the Griffin's destruction under a hail of the high-explosive shells.

Wolff didn't even have a speed advantage over his opponent. Even though the two ships had similar turbines, the Super Apache was a little faster than the bigger Griffin and accelerated quicker.

This was dogfighting at its finest as the two ships turned

and twisted in the sky, trying to gain the brief advantage that would mean the destruction of the other. And this was where Wolff had the advantage. Not only did he have more experience behind the controls of his gunship, he also had hundreds of hours in the cockpit of his personal Corsair, one of the best dogfighters that had ever been built. When it came to aerial dogfighting, there were few flyers who could play the game as well as the Wolfman.

At one point, Sloan used his greater speed to pull away from the Griffin. Zooming up to gain a thousand feet, he snapped the tail of his bird around to do a 180-degree turn and swooped back down on Wolff, his nose turret blazing. Wolff, however, simply wasn't there any more. The instant that he saw Sloan's tail come around, he rolled his ship over onto her side and, pulling maximum pitch to the rotor, flew sideways out of the path of the shells.

Snapping back, Wolff kicked down on his right rudder pedal and lined up for a fleeting shot. "Get 'em!"

Mojo triggered off a long burst as Sloan flashed by. He saw several of his HE shells explode harmlessly against the Super Apache's heavy armor plating, but the Apache was designed to stand up under heavy antiaircraft fire, not just criminals with assault rifles.

"I can't get at him!" the gunner shouted. "We don't have armor-piercing ammunition!"

"Try for his rotors!"

Wolff dumped his collective and dropped like a stone to follow Sloan as the Super Apache banked in the sky. Sloan had just set up for another gun run when suddenly he broke away. Pushing his ship's nose down, he headed for the base of the mountain.

"Rick!" Mojo shouted. "He's getting away!"

"The fuck he is!" Wolff banked sharply around and followed after the wildly gyrating gunship, his turbines screaming on overrev.

Hugging the mountainside, Sloan darted in and out of

the rock outcroppings and sped past the bowl on the side of the mountain where Wolff had stolen the chopper. Inside the Super Apache's cockpit, Sloan battled the strong winds whipping around the mountain. It was tricky flying, but if he could reach the safety of the forests and valleys on the other side of the peak, he could use his ship's greater speed to shake off the Griffin.

Wolff was hot on Sloan's tail, but wasn't gaining on him. Sloan dodged his gunship past a raging fire and ducked in low over one of the solar collectors. A sudden gust of wind caught his chopper and threw it to one side.

Instantly, he brought the ship back upright again, but the tip of one rotor blade sliced into the solar collector's fully charged capacitor. A blinding streak of lightning as bright as the laser beam leaped the length of the rotor blade as the ten thousand kilovolts stored in the giant capacitor discharged into the Super Apache.

The high-voltage charge flashed through the entire chopper, arcing between any gaps in the metal. Any space between a piece of metal that was not in direct contact with another was filled with the blue fire of electricity. Lightning bolts shot through the JP-4 fuel tanks in the armored belly of the gunship, instantly vaporizing the kerosene. The tank split open with the sudden pressure and sprayed JP-4 vapor into the interior of the ship. An electric arc ignited the vapor and the Super Apache exploded.

A ball of fire suddenly appeared in the sky where the Super Apache had been. Burning chunks of what had been a sleek flying machine flew through the air and slammed into the drifted snow banks below the mountain.

Wolff racked his Griffin around and came in low over the side of the mountain, but there was nothing to see. Sloan's chopper had completely disappeared. All that was left of the chopper and its pilot were hundreds of burning fragments fluttering down through the air.

Wolff keyed his throat mike. "Dragon Control, this is

Dragon Lead on board Dragon One Two," his voice sounded weary. "It's over. Let's go home."

Early the next morning, the men and women of Dragon Flight were packing up the CP at the Forest Service airstrip again. But this time they were definitely not dragging ass. Now that Wolff and Mugabe were back, they were in a hurry to get the hell out of this godforsaken frozen quagmire and get back to civilization. As far as they were concerned, even the Denver TPF headquarters would qualify as civilization. At least for now.

The only one who was not happy with the situation was Red. Supervising the move out was the least of his problems. He still had to recover the shattered wreckage of Gunner's Dragon One Four before they could go home. Gunner and Legs had survived the crash with only minor bruises, but their chopper was totally destroyed. Recovering the wreck and transporting the pieces back to Denver wouldn't be the end of it, either. When that was done, he would have to get two replacement ships checked out and on line before Dragon Flight would really be back on their feet and ready for duty. And that was not going to be fun.

Even with the full maintenance facilities and crew at the Denver base working on it, he was looking at a minimum of two weeks before they would be done. And that was only if the two replacement ships didn't arrive with a long list of deficiencies that had to be corrected before he could park them out on the flight line. As far as Red was concerned, this whole thing had been an unmitigated disaster, and he was looking for someone, anyone, to blame it on.

Wolff and Mugabe, however, were not candidates for Red's displeasure. After splashing that Super Apache, their shit didn't stink around the TPF. Their last-minute save of the Diablo Canyon nuclear power plant was considered to have been the best piece of work in the entire history of the

TPF, and they had been put in for the highest awards for valor in the force. Red would rather have put a boot up their asses for getting shot down in the first place and causing all of this, but he knew that he couldn't do that to the two newest national heros, the men who had singlehandedly saved Southern California from nuclear destruction.

Red didn't think it was all that big a deal, though. He had been to Southern California and considered it a cesspool. As far as he was concerned, everything south of the Bay Area could slip away from the rest of the United States and fall into the sea. But even he had to admit that a nuclear explosion would have made a real mess of things.

The fate of California, however, had nothing to do with packing up and getting the hell out of this place. He shifted the dead cigar to the other side of his mouth and went to see if those fumble-fingered morons he had for recovery mechanics had gotten the slings rigged properly yet.

The first of the C-9s was on the strip and a line of men steadily handed boxes up into the open rear ramp door. Buzz and Wolff stood outside the door of the commo tent and watched the loading process.

"Have they figured out what in the hell this was all about yet?" Wolff asked.

"The air force and TPF investigation teams are still sorting through the mess," he said. "But they think they know most of it."

"What in the hell did Sloan think he was doing, anyway?" Wolff asked. "What did he have to gain by blowing up a nuke plant?"

"It's a little complicated," Buzz replied. "But most of it centers around his company SOLCO. He had invested a lot of Mob money in it and he was not selling enough solar collectors to make it pay off. The Mob was calling in their markers and Sloan figured that if a nuke plant blew up, the st of them would be outlawed immediately and create an stant market for solar energy."

"But what was all this about running for office?"

"We're still sorting through his campaign records, but it oks like that was primarily financed by the Mob as well. hey wanted to move their operations into the Sun Belt, ad he was supposed to make it easier for them when he got to office."

"I'll bet there were a lot of red faces among the people ho supported him," Wolff grinned. "When they found out at they were supporting organized crime."

"They're going to be more than a little embarrassed," uzz said. "The IRS is looking into the funding of the lean Earth party, and some of those people are going to ad themselves in deep kimchi before this is all over."

Wolff shook his head. "What a hell of a way to start the w year."

"The new millennium, you mean."

"That too," Wolff agreed. "With this kind of beginning, I onder what's going to happen next?"

Buzz thought for a moment. "Well," he said, "I hope that e can go back to routine law enforcement for awhile. This ving the world stuff is getting a little old."

Wolff smiled, "You got that right, sir. But popping run--the-mill maggots and drug dealers is going to be a little me after all this excitement."

Buzz shook his head. "I don't think it'll be too tame. You d your buddy always seem to be able to find something citing."

"Speaking of Mojo," Wolff asked, "what's the latest on his m?" Mugabe had been airlifted with Zoomie's casualties m the firefight at the mountain and was in the hospital in enver.

"It looks like all he needs is two weeks in a cast," Buzz id, "and he'll be back for duty."

"Good," Wolff said. "He'll be back in time to help me

check out the new Dragon One Zero. Red should have i ready by then."

"You two cowboys had better take better care of that new bird than you did the last one or Red's going to tear you tw new assholes."

Wolff grinned. "You know Red, he's all bark and no . .

"Wolff!" Red's voice bellowed from behind him. "Get you ass over here. Just because you're a hotshot pilot doesn mean that you can stand around all day jacking your jaw while everyone else is working."

Buzz smiled. "You're right, he's all bark."

"And, Captain," Red continued. "As soon as you can se your way clear to quit talking and get your stuff together we can load it on the plane. Sir!"

Buzz shrugged. "Guess he's got some teeth after all."